Nowadays and Lonelier

Nowadays and Lonelier

stories

Carmella Gray-Cosgrove

ARSENAL PULP PRESS
VANCOUVER

NOWADAYS AND LONELIER
Copyright © 2021 by Carmella Gray-Cosgrove

ARSENAL PULP PRESS
Suite 202 – 211 East Georgia St.
Vancouver, BC V6A 1Z6
Canada
arsenalpulp.com

The publisher gratefully acknowledges the support of the Canada Council for the Arts and the British Columbia Arts Council for its publishing program, and the Government of Canada, and the Government of British Columbia (through the Book Publishing Tax Credit Program), for its publishing activities.

Arsenal Pulp Press acknowledges the xʷməθkʷəy̓əm (Musqueam), Sḵwx̱wú7mesh (Squamish), and səl̓ilwətaʔɬ (Tsleil-Waututh) Nations, custodians of the traditional, ancestral, and unceded territories where our office is located. We pay respect to their histories, traditions, and continuous living cultures and commit to accountability, respectful relations, and friendship.

This is a work of fiction. Any resemblance of characters to persons either living or deceased is purely coincidental.

Previously published:
"Almost Touching," *New Quarterly*, Issue 158, Spring 2021
"Another Angel," as "The Annunciation," *Antigonish Review*, Issue 200
"The Cull," *Riddle Fence*, Issue 26
"The Dance of the Cygnets," *PRISM international*, SPRAWL (58.3), Spring 2020
"Float," *Riddle Fence*, Issue 36
"La Foule," as "The Painter," *Acta Victoriana* (144.2)
"Nowadays and Lonelier," *FreeFall Magazine* (XXX.1), Spring 2020
"Power Pose," *Riddle Fence*, Issue 37
"Warmer Soon," *Broken Pencil* (online), November 19, 2019

Cover and text design by Jazmin Welch
Cover art by Janice Wu, *Matchsticks*, 2015, 15″ × 20″, pencil and gouache on paper
Edited by Shirarose Wilensky
Proofread by Alison Strobel

Printed and bound in Canada

Library and Archives Canada Cataloguing in Publication:
Title: Nowadays and lonelier : stories / Carmella Gray-Cosgrove.
Names: Gray-Cosgrove, Carmella, author.
Identifiers: Canadiana (print) 20210216050 | Canadiana (ebook) 20210216123 | ISBN 9781551528717 (softcover) | ISBN 9781551528724 (HTML)
Classification: LCC PS8613.R38925 N69 2021 | DDC C813/.6—dc23

For David Mandville

Contents

The Dance
of the Cygnets

Ballet class starts at eight a.m., so I get up early. In the bathroom while I shower I can hear my neighbour slam their bathroom
door and puke into the toilet. I hear them puking every morning, a
deep heave and then a splash. After my shower I bobby-pin my hair
into a bun and pull on my tights and leotard, then my clothes. I try to
eat breakfast, but it's too early, and listening to the puking has turned
my stomach. I drink my coffee quickly, black, throw a hard-boiled egg
in my bag. The hallway outside my apartment smells like steamed
broccoli but slightly off, an undertone of rot. The smell starts as soon
as you open the apartment door, and it travels throughout the building, with a definitive crescendo on the third floor. It becomes faint
as you walk from the elevator down the hall to the lobby but is only
fully gone again when you step outside the building.

On the commute I've been listening to an audiobook about
trees. Apparently, there is this white stringy fungus in the root systems of forests, and even in more dispersed groups of trees like in a

park or a neighbourhood. The fungus connects the forest into one sentient community. It's called a mycorrhizal network. It's underneath us most of the time, filaments that reach out for each other deep underground. A hidden conversation. The fungus is in a symbiotic relationship with the trees—if the forest thrives, the fungus thrives—but it is also somehow part of the forest's brain. When a tree is about to die, it releases all the nutrients stored in its trunk and branches down to its roots, and the network of fungus transmits all that sap to trees that need it. The fungus knows where there is less water in the forest and helps the trees transport the sap to that area. Like an egalitarian redistribution of wealth, or one unified body.

I call my sister, Sandy, on the walk from the bus to the SkyTrain. I plan it so the call will be short—there is no reception once I go down the escalator. Sandy almost died and is in the hospital, but we don't talk about that. On the phone, she asks about Rita, a dancer in my program I told Sandy about because I'm jealous of her. Everyone at the ballet school is much smaller than me. Tiny, beautiful girls from rich families with delicate arched feet and bony legs. They have perfect little bulges of muscle for calves and quads and hamstrings, and their stomachs are concave. Rita is the most perfect of all of them. She's from Seattle and is very elegant, always smells like lavender oil, and basically only eats celery sticks and salads. I don't have anything to say about Rita today: I've already told Sandy how she washes her face with Cetaphil at lunchtime and reads romance novels in her sweatpants as she stretches before class. Rita is first cast for Odette in the production of *Swan Lake* we're rehearsing for our year-end showcase. I am second cast as one of the cygnets—the four swans who link arms and trot around really fast twitching their heads in circles, and I have a part in the corps. Everyone loves the "Dance of the Cygnets," but I would way rather do one of Odette's slow solos. We have to learn all the parts in our repertoire class, though, so I still get to dance Odette, even if I don't ever get to do it onstage.

My sister is actually my twin. Not identical. She hates ballet and she looks nothing like me. She's into video games, snowboarding, self-harm, and hallucinogens. She fell off the roof of our school in grade twelve when she was high on mushrooms and tore the tip of her thumb off on the way down. Caught on a nail. She was otherwise unscathed. She has a line of thin vertical scars around her hips that run beneath the waistline of her pants in a perfectly spaced row. Tidy veins of raised white where she carved into herself with a sharp knife. She's a ski bum in Whistler now. Or she was until last week. She even calls herself that. She loves hearing about Rita, I think, because she likes it when she knows I feel insecure. Like it reassures her that there are lots of people out there who are better than me and that she is on the better path in life. She has always been like that. Helping me tear myself down so she can rise up. Even though her up is always assisted by something. Coke most often, but speed, too, and crack in a pinch.

I haven't told her that I'm the only person in our class who can do Odette's double rond de jambe développés in the Odette solo without faltering. That's one of the solos with the two rows of swans on either side of Odette while she is doing this amazing adage. Double rond de jambe and développé seconde, arms up, chassé, tendue arrière, double rond de jambe and développé seconde, arms up, chassé, tendue arrière, double rond de jambe and développé seconde, arms up and bourrée, bourrée, bourrée, piqué turn.

"I'm at the escalator," I say to Sandy, which cues the end of the conversation.

I turn the audiobook back on for the ride on the SkyTrain and keep listening as I walk up Granville with my toes pointed out. I am still thinking about the trees as I do my warm-up in the studio. Leg swings to loosen my hip joints, downward dog to stretch out my spine, ankle rolls to wake up my feet. Squeezing swollen, blistered feet into your pointe shoes at 7:45 a.m. is one of the most unpleasant sensations I can think of. Each point of contact between raw toe joint and cold hard canvas prickles an objection. I think about the dying trees dropping all their sap, and then I just think about dying. I think about dying a lot. Not my own death, really, though sometimes that, too. And not in a suicidal kind of way. More of a musing on nothingness and the state of being blank. Sometimes I wish I could be blank. My pointe shoes squeak against the Marley flooring as I relevé in first and lower down slowly over and over, the rosin on the tips of my shoes leaving smudges of white on the floor.

Sandy hasn't told our mom what happened. Mom lives in Norway—that's where she's from. She came to Vancouver when she was eighteen for university and to smoke pot, met our dad, and then dropped out when she got pregnant. Sandy says she's had a taste for drugs since birth because Mom and Dad spent that first year together in an acid-fuelled stupor. Sandy's joking when she says that, but Mom feels guilty enough that there were never any consequences for Sandy getting high when we were teenagers. It always felt like

Mom was just biding her time before she went home. Like she was waiting for us to be able to take care of ourselves so she could remove herself from the messed-up equation that is our family. Then she met Andreas online and she was out of here a week after we graduated from high school.

Mom paid for our plane tickets to visit her last summer. On the last day of our trip, we ended up at a mausoleum. It was amazing in there. This dark room with a low, heavy door you have to bow to get through and at first you can't see anything because there's not much light, but as your eyes adjust, these dark paintings on the walls start to emerge, illuminated by dim spotlights. It's all painted in rusty browns and blacks, dark greys and reds, and the lights are amber, giving everything a warm glow. The ceiling is high and arched. It's just one room and the paintings go from floor to ceiling to floor again. They're all of bodies. Bodies having sex and giving birth and dying. As your eyes adjust to the dark you see more and more bodies, some all knotted together in these mosh pits of suffering, some in ecstatic orgies, and this one woman standing surrounded by hundreds of babies, with one clutched high on her shoulder out of everyone's reach, her head pressed into its little body.

Someone had brought their toddler, and you're supposed to be completely quiet in the mausoleum because the acoustics are so intense in there, but the toddler kept making these cooing noises that bounced around the walls like Ping-Pong balls. It was majestic. Sandy and I were awed. It was one of the only times we've loved the same thing. The artist had his ashes placed in an urn above the low door so that as you stoop to exit the mausoleum, you're bowing to him. Sandy and I thought that was hilariously egotistical.

I like to imagine what it would look like if all the bodies in those paintings could move and dance, pulsating together in their erotic life cycle. There's no room for that type of movement in *Swan Lake*, even though it's about all the same shit. Love and sex and death. I love *Swan Lake* in a different way. For all its rigidity and technique. And I love a white tutu.

On my way home from class I am caked in sweat. Today we worked on *The Dying Swan*. Despite what most people think, *The Dying Swan* solo is not actually from *Swan Lake*. It's a separate solo that was made specifically for a Russian ballerina, Anna Pavlova, who performed it over and over for her whole life. Perpetual death. But we're including it in the showcase anyway, because it's the most dramatic death scene in classical ballet. I stare at my reflection in the window on the SkyTrain and the bags under my eyes make me look like I have empty sockets. Pas de bourrée, bourrée, bourrée, piqué arabesque, piqué attitude, fouetté to attitude, turn, à terre, you're sad, front leg out and bend over slow, rond de jambe à terre to back bend, then up, relevé attitude, turn, piqué, bourrée, bourrée, bourrée, quick arms then melt, bourrée, dangle, bourrée, you're dying, bourrée, sink down, bourrée, bourrée.

I notice my lips moving in the reflection in the window and my arms are twitching, marking out the steps. Bourrées are the worst when you have blisters and your feet aren't fully warmed up yet. You're up en pointe and your feet are tight in fifth position and you take these impossibly small steps, keeping your feet sucked together and bending your knees just a bit. Bourrée means stuffed, and you are. Your feet are all stuffed up in your shoes and your legs are glued together. It can also mean drunk. But I'd like to see a drunk try that. And while your feet are taking those microscopic steps, grinding your toes over and over into the box of your pointe shoes with the weight of your whole body bearing down on them, your arms and back are supposed to be weightless, moving smooth and serene like nothing is happening down there at all. Meanwhile, the skin on your big toe is tearing and your bunions are being forced sideways and the liquid between your toe joints is being squished out so your bones are grinding against each other, almost guaranteeing that you'll have arthritis when you're old. The dying swan does a lot of bourrées. Like it's her penance to suffer in these, her last moments on Earth.

When we were twelve, our dad died of a heroin overdose. At the reception I stood at the table with the sandwiches, tuna salad in one hand and egg salad in the other, looking at the incredible glossiness of my patent leather shoes. It wasn't like he was really involved in our lives or anything anyway. Before he moved out he would give us pony rides on his back—Sandy and I would be up there yelling, "Yeehaw!" and whoever was sitting in the back would slap his butt to go faster. When I was in the back I would wrap my arms around Sandy, press my cheek against her spine, listen to her heart pound against her ribs, and hang on for dear life. That's how it has always felt with Sandy. Like I'm hanging on for dear life.

After our dad left, we didn't see him for years. He died in a hotel you can live in, like a cheap apartment with no kitchen and no lease, that also rented rooms by the hour, with a woman who was passed out when the paramedics showed up. It's unclear which type of tenants they were. The woman lived. She didn't come to the funeral, which was at a church Dad went to for meals and sometimes to get some sleep. The reverend knew him and came to talk to me after the service. He said my dad was a lost soul in life and that I could take comfort in knowing that now he was at peace. At that time I had mild acne on my forehead, not big pustules but small pimples I would pick at when I was anxious. I had gone at them the night before and had an explosion of swollen dots on my face. At some point during the reception my aunt told me that when you pop a zit you get puss in all the surrounding pores and that was why I had so many. I felt guilty every time I popped a zit after that, like I was bringing the bane of pimples upon myself with my habit.

I don't remember my mom at the funeral, but she must have been there, and I don't remember crying. I remember Sandy, though, silent like I had never seen her before. She stood next to me as everyone milled around the reception hall, slipped her hand into mine, soft and clammy. There were lots of people we didn't know, lots of poor people who looked like they were just there for the sandwiches, but in retrospect, they were probably my dad's friends from that neighbourhood. Bourrée, dangle, bourrée, you're dying, bourrée, sink down, bourrée, bourrée.

When I open the door to my apartment building there is the smell of broccoli. Up the elevator, it's stronger, down the hall, it's fading, into the apartment, it's gone.

I get up extra early this morning so I can shower before my neighbour's puking starts. Today I am going to have an extra cup of coffee and be sharp in ballet class. I am going to have a perfect bun, and if we're doing Odette's solo in repertoire, I am going to nail every single one of those double rond de jambes. I am going to have the most controlled relevé anyone has ever seen. And my arms are gonna float like goddamn clouds during my bourrées. If we're doing the "Dance of the Cygnets," my feet are gonna be a blur, perfectly pointed and sharp, and I will land every sauté on the beat.

On the bus I put my headphones on and I manage to get a seat. I am listening to the book about the trees to stop the steps from the "Dance of the Cygnets" from running through my head. The "Dance of the Cygnets" is supposed to emulate the way baby swans cluster and move as a jumpy, pecking unit. They're busy and tight together, scared maybe, cold, hearts racing, moving where the others pull. In the dance they're supposed to be learning to fly and there is a slow build. It starts with these dainty trotting coupés from side to side, legs low, feet scooping up to the ankle. The music starts out really staccato and kind of quiet, mostly horns. Then it gets busier and the violins take over from the horns as the legs get a bit higher. The extra coffee has made me zippy. Coupé, coupé, coupé, coupé, coupé, coupé, coupé, coupé, jeté, pas de bourrée, relevé switch sides. As the music builds, the steps get bolder and the baby swans start to jump, legs lifting up to the knee. Entrechat quatre passé, entrechat quatre passé, échappé, échappé, échappé, échappé. I am willing the audiobook to drown out the swans.

The book is on this chapter about a forest in Utah called Pando. It's a forest of trembling aspens and they're all clones of one another and share one enormous root system that's 80,000 years old. Pando is the oldest living organism on Earth, and it seems to be dying. No one is exactly sure why, but they think it's some combination of drought and fire suppression. Trembling aspens love fire. Fire makes it so other types of trees are wiped out from the underbrush and baby Pando clones can sprout up from their ashes, which infuse the soil with micronutrients and nurture perfect saplings. Just as the book is telling me about the baby clones being born like phoenixes from fire, the narration stops abruptly and my phone starts ringing into my headphones. It's Sandy. She is never the one to call, it's always me. But everything with Sandy is different since the accident last week. Though I'm not sure it can be called an accident. I decline the call and wait for the book to cut back in. Relevé arabesque, fondu, coupé, relevé arabesque, fondu, coupé, relevé arabesque, fondu, coupé. The phone starts ringing again and I answer.

"Are you screening my calls?" Sandy asks.

Coupé, coupé, coupé, coupé, jeté, coupé, relevé écarté.

"I need to talk," she says.

Sandy jumped off the Lions Gate Bridge in a psychotic break brought on by too much cocaine.

"They are feeding me the shittiest food and I am not allowed to have a cigarette," she says.

She drove down from Whistler at two a.m., high as a kite, pulled over in the middle of the bridge, and jumped over the side. Somehow, she did not die. Relevé arabesque, fondu, coupé.

"I want a grilled cheese," she says.

Jeté, coupé, relevé écarté.

"The nurses suck here. Are you even listening to me?" she asks.

The hardest part of the "Dance of the Cygnets" is the fifteen pas de chats starting from upstage right and travelling across all in perfect unison. Pas de chat means "step of the cat," and they are these jumps where you tuck one foot up to your crotch and then the other so there is a moment where you're suspended with both legs bent up under you and then you land your feet in quick succession.

"I keep waking up thinking I'm in the ocean," she says.

Fifteen pas de chats in a row with your arms linked with three other people is hard. Today we're probably going to practise this sequence over and over so it's smooth and our tutus bounce at the exact same time.

"They say I'm in withdrawal, but they have me on such a cocktail of things that I can't feel it," she says.

Pas de chat, pas de chat, pas de chat, pas de chat, pas de chat, pas de chat, pas de chat, pas de chat. Pando reminds me of the four cygnets. Tree clones and baby swans. Things that are the same as other things but somehow are still their own entities.

"I didn't realize what I was doing until I felt the water. It hurt so bad, like the worst bellyflop, and then like when you hold an ice cube for too long and the bones in your fingers ache," she says.

The bus is at my stop. The fungus in the tree roots of a forest is hollow, they say. Like blood vessels. All a tree can do on its own is turn carbon dioxide from the air into sugar. I get off and walk to the SkyTrain with my phone held out in front of me.

"I regretted it as soon as I hit the water. And I kept thinking about you and how mad you would be," she says.

Seven more pas de chats. Pas de chat, pas de chat, pas de chat, pas de chat, pas de chat, pas de chat, pas de chat. This is Sandy apologizing. The fungus needs the sugar that the trees make from carbon dioxide in order to exist and grow. In return, the fungus gets minerals from the earth and transmits them to the tree roots so the tree can keep living and keep making sugar for the fungus to keep growing.

"Do you think that's how dad felt? Do you think he was thinking about us?" she asks.

The last sequence in the "Dance of the Cygnets" is beautiful. It's fifteen emboîtés, which are these fast, tight kicks alternating left and right out to the front. Emboîté means boxed in. It's the cygnets' final confinement. You do the emboîtés over and over until your thighs burn and your palms are aching from clutching each other so tightly, but then suddenly you break away and you're not holding hands anymore. You feel the air between your fingers as you piqué arabesque and you're free, no longer a cygnet. The sweat on your hands makes them feel cool as you sweep your arms up above your head.

"I'm at the escalator," I say.

Nowadays and Lonelier

A story about a family's former babysitter who is a Jehovah's Witness. Years after she has stopped babysitting for them, she cold-calls the mother and sets up a date to visit. When she shows up she is wheeling an overnight bag behind her. It clacks over the threshold.

A story that culminates in a car accident between a funeral procession and a young couple.

A story about a city that is overrun with war memorials to the point that it's hard to move through the streets because the statues are so close together. A forest of hard bronze men holding rifles in various positions.

The young couple in the car accident are fooling around when they crash into the funeral procession on the bridge. Lou is driving. Daria is going down on him, the emergency brake digging into her ribs as she leans over from the passenger seat.

A story about a man who is dying and wants to tell his son that he is adopted, but the man's ex-wife does not want him to tell. His dying has made him concerned about honesty, about going to the grave with a secret in his heart that is heavy from knowing his days with his son are numbered. His ex-wife thinks they should leave well enough alone. The man's name is Saul and his ex-wife's name is Enid.

The Jehovah's Witness babysitter has been through a recent divorce, she tells the mother and daughter over coffee in the living room. Her hair is smooth and black, newly greying at the temples. They are sitting on the pink jacquard couch. She still hasn't opened the suitcase, and the mother wonders momentarily if she is going to ask to stay with them.

The man who is dying, Saul, has stage four colon cancer and has decided to try naturopathic remedies instead of conventional cancer treatments. These include: frequent CBD enemas, a concentrated turmeric tincture, intravenous vitamin C, and acupuncture. Apart from the cancer, Saul is healthy. He has olive skin and thick brown hair. His eyes are the colour of a heath.

A story about an old woman who wants to have her ashes compressed into a diamond when she dies. Princess cut, or perhaps marquise, she thinks. She has very thin hair and a shiny scalp. She is obsessed with her possessions like Mrs Gereth in the Henry James novel *The Spoils of Poynton*, but nowadays and lonelier.

While Daria is giving Lou road head, before he crashes, she can smell the sweat on his pubes. The smell is stale and sour, repulsive in fact, and she thinks about how, actually, she would rather not be giving him head.

On the pink jacquard couch, the babysitter sips her coffee in silence. She sets her mug down on the coffee table from Pier 1 Imports and, with a deep breath, gestures to the suitcase. It turns out the whole visit has been a ruse to sell the mother and daughter skin care products as part of a pyramid scheme. Maybe it's Mary Kay or Rodan + Fields.

A story about a young woman who is stranded on an ice pan and floats into the harbour just north of St. John's. She keeps herself alive in the rank, but warm, carcass of a seal.

A story set at a family reunion, told from the perspective of a little girl. She is wearing flowing floral-print pants and a white blouse with flared sleeves. She and her cousin order soft-core porn off pay-per-view in his parents' hotel room.

Saul's naturopathic therapies aren't working and he starts chemo-therapy, but at this point it is just to buy some extra time. He still hasn't told his son that he is not his biological father. If Saul were to tell him, he would reassure him that he still thinks of himself as his father and loves him very much.

The girl who the Jehovah's Witness babysitter used to babysit is now a teenager. When she was a kid she would often wonder about blood transfusions and half a fact about the religion that she picked up from a conversation she didn't quite understand. She understood enough, however, to worry that the babysitter would die if she ever had an accident.

Lou crashes into the funeral procession partly because he is high, and partly because he is coming, and it feels so good that he closes his eyes, lifts his face to the sky. It is a goddamn holy experience. He feels the crunch of metal through his legs as his spine whips forward. The car veers and his foot hits the brake before there's a second crunch into a guardrail.

Saul dies a month after he starts chemo and does not tell his son about the adoption and that he is not his biological father before he goes.

The little girl at the family reunion looks in the mirror in her aunt's hotel room and admires the beautiful flared sleeves of her shirt. Runs her finger over the pearl buttons down its front. She puts two butterfly clips in her bangs to keep them off her forehead, squeezes the hinge open, and then lets go. The teeth scrape through her hair.

The old woman with the shiny scalp keeps her valuable jewellery in the toes of her shoes which are wrapped in tissue in their original boxes on shelves in the bottom of her closet. Every day she checks in each pair to makes sure it's all still there. She used to have a cleaning lady, Pat, who stole her opal ring and her KitchenAid mixer. The old woman has been vigilant ever since.

If Enid tells her son about the adoption, she also must tell him that it happened overseas and that he may never be able to find his biological parents. That the record keeping at the agency had been careless at best.

The teenager still wonders about blood transfusions. Can you change your mind on your deathbed and get the transfusion? If you do change your mind, do you still get to be a Jehovah's Witness? Maybe it's like Catholicism, with some system of repentance and forgiveness. Or maybe it is harsher. Maybe the choice really is between death and salvation or life and damnation.

The city has so many war memorials because the government is mostly old men who love war history, and as a result, it's easier for artists to get funding for war memorials than avant-garde sculpture.

Lou cums in Daria's mouth and when the car crunches into the hearse the jolt is unexpected and she spits as a reflex. She didn't mean to. Her head is momentarily wedged in Lou's lap, between the steering wheel and his stomach.

As the ice pan moves within sight of the shore the young woman looks out of the seal carcass periodically and scans for signs of people. The ocean spray stings her face.

The little girl is still admiring her flared sleeves as she holds the remote and flicks through the channels with her cousin, Stefan. The family reunion is in Harrison Hot Springs and people have come from all over Canada and the States. Stefan is two years older and is just entering puberty.

It is not a serious car accident and no one is killed. Lou and Daria are unscathed, though humiliated. The dead person in the hearse remains dead.

The diamond dinner ring is in the old woman's beige Clarks. She holds it to the light and it glints. The emerald earrings are in her blue Skechers. They are the green of a crystalline ocean. The fresh-water pearl pendant is in her suede Hush Puppies, iridescent, with a wrinkle at the top.

The girl's sleeve rests just over her wrist bone and the bottom of the flare dangles down. She feels like a princess from the story "The Twelve Dancing Princesses."

Don't get me wrong: there is a time and a place for a good war memorial. But this has gotten a bit extreme.

In the seal, the young woman floats past an outport community at night and can see the lights twinkling in the frost, puffs of smoke from chimneys like the nativity scene on her grandmother's piano at Christmas.

The babysitter massages Active Hydration Body Replenish cream into the teenager's palm, sliding her hands up her forearm, making circles on the dry skin of her elbow.

As the little girl flicks channels she comes to several that say you have to order that channel separately. The shows on these channels have really great names like *Secrets of a French Maid* and *Fruits of Passion.*

When you walk through the streets, sometimes you have to turn sideways to avoid the tip of a bronze bayonet.

The old woman puts each jewel back in its shoe, each shoe in its box, each box back on the shelf. Her index finger roots toward the toes of the next pair. There is a faint smell of sweat and lavender-scented baking soda.

Careless record keeping would be an understatement, Enid thinks. Two years prior to Saul's death, she learned that the adoption agency had been accused of gross negligence and shut down.

Sometimes you have to twist around the bronze corner of a soldier's jacket slung over a tired shoulder. The war has just ended and he is hot. With his opposite hand he wipes his brow forevermore with a bronze hanky.

The woman in the seal carcass is finally spotted by the coast guard.

As the babysitter rubs circles with the moisturizer over the teenager's elbow, the teenager is thinking about when she kissed her best friend, Claire, at a sleepover. She closes her eyes for just a second, imagines it's Claire stroking her elbow.

Stefan dares his younger cousin to press Order on a movie called *Bedtime Stories: Another Woman.*

The old woman wonders if her husband will also want his ashes turned into a diamond. She has not asked him and suspects he would not understand the question at this point, as he has dementia and is living in an old folks' home called Meadowbrook Seniors Residence.

Sometimes you have to duck under the bronze elbow, right at eye level, of a soldier in salute.

The mother reads the back of one of the bottles. "How much for the dermabrasion cream?" she asks.

Daria squeezes her head out from between the steering wheel and Lou's stomach, and Lou zips up his fly quickly as she moves back to her seat, wiping her mouth and fastening her seat belt.

In fact, Enid had learned that the children from the adoption agency had, in some cases, been taken from their families without just cause. It had come to light that the agency had been destroying records to obfuscate possible legal action.

The young woman is very cold and when she sees the coast guard boat she sticks her arm out from the seal carcass and waves frantically.

Once, a bronze artist proposed an art installation that was basically a giant vagina opening up to the ocean. He said that the negative space was a codfish, but really, when you look at it, you can tell that it is a vagina.

Stefan moves a pillow over his lap. On the TV, a redhead in a black satin bodysuit that might as well be a thong in front stands in a doorway fondling the seam on her hip. She raises her hand seductively on the door frame. The little girl is staring intently at the woman as Stefan reaches his hand under the pillow.

Enid is left with a difficult decision.

A replacement hearse comes to the scene of the accident and continues on to the cemetery with the coffin, the body, and the procession.

The city made an exception for the codfish sculpture, but once it was clear that it was actually a vagina, they became even firmer in their convictions about war memorials.

When she realizes that the coast guard might not see her, the young woman crawls out of the seal carcass and starts yelling and jumping up and down on the ice pan.

As the old woman fingers the freshwater pearl pendant, hands chalky from the lavender baking soda, she decides she will have her husband's ashes made into a diamond, even though, when he was still able to make legal decisions, he expressly requested a corporeal interment, in writing, in his will.

Enid has decided, once again, against telling her son about the adoption.

Daria and Lou do not tell the cops that she was giving him road head. Instead, Lou says that he had been texting and didn't notice the procession.

No one lives in the city anymore, as there is no longer any space for parking or driving or cafés or restaurants. But all the men who died in the war are there again in bronze, and that makes everyone happy.

The teenager remembers that it is not Claire who is stroking her elbow and opens her eyes. Her cheeks are flushed. "The dermabrasion cream is forty dollars," says the babysitter, who has not noticed that the teenager is trying to pull her arm away.

As the young woman jumps on the ice pan, water splashes up over her feet and the seal lolls to and fro.

Unfortunately for Enid, she has overlooked the fact that Saul's brother and his wife know that the son is adopted, and they have told Saul's brother's wife's brother about the infertility and the trip overseas. Saul's brother's wife's brother is not very good at keeping secrets.

Lou hopes the cops won't check his phone to see if he was actually texting. He hopes they won't notice the zipper imprint on Daria's cheek.

Saul's brother's wife's brother tells his niece, who is also Saul's niece, that her cousin, Saul's son, is not actually, biologically speaking, her cousin when she mentions anxiety over a dream in which she French kissed her cousin, Saul's son.

Lou gets a $225 ticket for texting while driving and six points on his licence. Daria decides she really does not like giving head and will not be doing it anymore.

The mother buys the dermabrasion cream as well as a foaming sunless tan mousse and an active hydration serum. She e-transfers $130 to the babysitter, whose email address is *godsparadise144@marykay.com*, or maybe *redemptionforthefew@rodanandfields.com*.

Saul's niece tells her cousin, Saul's son, that she dreamt about French kissing him.

The coast guard guys are called Alex and Dean. They are dressed from head to toe in safety orange, and as Alex pulls the Zodiac up to the ice pan with the seal rocking back and forth, the filthy young woman has tears streaming down her face. Under his breath, Alex says to Dean, "What the fuck is going on here?"

Saul's niece also tells her cousin, Saul's son, that they could French kiss in real life if he wants. Because he is not, biologically speaking, her cousin.

Mars Spills Out

You were always finding injured birds. A crow with a broken leg, a seagull coated in oil, a baby chickadee fallen out of its nest and abandoned, a starling attacked by the neighbour's cat, a stunned hummingbird under the window, a chicken escaped off the back of the truck headed to the slaughterhouse. You brought the birds home wrapped in your jean jacket or, if they were small, cupped in your hands.

I am eight and the route for the chicken truck passes right in front of our apartment, a basement suite just south of Hastings with a chain-link fence around our patch of yard and the mountains looming tall above the low buildings across the alley. Even if you don't see the truck pass, you can smell the stench of chicken shit and fear. The saddest smell in the world, you say. You're coming home with groceries and you see the chicken tumble off the back of the truck, and then squawk frantically down the road. You put your bags down and outrun it, tuck it like a football under your arm, cover its eyes so it goes still. Your bangs stick with sweat to your forehead. The chicken is so unhealthy it looks like it has already been plucked. A lone row of feathers around its neck, a meagre tail. But it's cocky as anything. You say it knows it has defied fate. It struts around the living room for weeks, perked up on its new diet of fresh fruit and love, before we drive it to a petting zoo in Chilliwack on a warm Sunday.

They follow me now, years later—injured birds. I find them wherever they are. This strange gift passed down from you. A yellow-breasted chat, stunned outside the auditorium on the first day of high school after homeroom. A disoriented junco outside the arts building in my first year of university. A one-legged finch beside the Student Union Building the next. A falcon in the middle of the highway halfway across the country.

You tell me that if I ever take up smoking, you'll kill yourself. I'm fifteen at a Halloween party in a basement in Kerrisdale. I'm wearing a bright red taffeta eighties prom dress, doing shots of vodka from Chelsea's cleavage. The taffeta makes my thighs itch and I try to scratch inconspicuously. I pass out briefly on the bathroom floor and wake up to Chelsea sitting on the toilet with her legs spread and her boyfriend going down on her. I eat a tab of acid and gaze in the mirror as my tiara spills off my head and my whole face is encrusted in rhinestones. Someone calls you at four in the morning to come pick me up. You drive the half-hour to that side of town to storm the basement like a Fury. But there is only pity as you haul me to the car, my arm draped over your shoulder, your arm around my hip, hugging layers of crinoline.

I am five when your dad dies. At the wake, his hands are clasped in front of him in the casket. Someone has placed a large prismed amethyst between them, pointing up. When you bring me up to pay our respects, you see the crystal and begin to laugh hysterically. Tears stream down your face. You gasp for air as you try to inhale. You hold my hand as you excuse us and we leave. That spring, a robin flies into our living room, through the open patio door. I come home from school and we sit watching it. It stays all evening, cocking its head, hopping from chair to couch to chair. You make supper and talk to it from the kitchen. You tell me that it is the reincarnation of your father. You apologize to the robin for the laughing fit. It chirps loudly and leaves at sunset. It comes back every spring for five years.

I am eight and I cry when you leave for your night shifts. Emotions so big I can't recall feeling that sense of loss as an adult for anything less than death. As you get ready, I plead with you to stay, thinking maybe you'll realize how cruel it is. It feels like my whole body will collapse from the tragedy of being away from you. I cry myself to sleep, clutching a picture of you I've taken from the photo album, imagining you are gone forever. It isn't until I have a child many years later that I find those emotions again. Looking down at him in my arms and aching with missing him, even though he is right there, tight against my chest. For months after I give birth you come every morning to hold the baby while I shower and drink coffee. You crawl into my bed next to him and I crawl out, naked and exhausted.

I am six when we move out of the city for a year on a whim and up the coast, a ferry ride, another drive. You tell me we have to leave my dad behind so he can keep his job. He visits on weekends and every Sunday is a flood of tears as he gets on the boat back to the city. One night I wake to you standing at the window in my bedroom, staring at the sky. "Look," you say, gesturing frantically. "A UFO." I stand beside you, holding on to your nightie, gazing at the stars. You find a baby chickadee at the base of a tree. You wait and watch, just in case, but its mother doesn't come back. You watch until the baby gets lethargic and woozy, and then you can't wait anymore and take it inside. You hold it gently and place it in a cardboard box on a heating pad set to low. You feed it every two hours all night. But in the morning it is weak and trembling. It won't eat off the chopsticks you've been using to drop wet dog food into its beak. It dies in that nest alone, your hand resting next to its frail body.

In college I fall in love with J. He lives with his girlfriend in Richmond and loves Woody Allen movies. If I were to meet him now, both these facts would make him instantly repellent. I watch *Annie Hall* alone in my room and text him that I am Diane and he is Woody. Which isn't far off. The age difference between J and me fits Allen's track record. He is short and not as ugly as Woody Allen. I am tall and less cute than Diane Keaton. It seems like a sweet comparison to me then.

J and I are lying on the grass after English. It's almost the end of the semester. My best friend Kate died recently. I'm reading a book of poems by Dylan Thomas my dad gave me and I tell J how beautiful they are. He tells me I better not be thinking of reading him poetry and I laugh. "Of course not," I say. "Never."

I am sixteen and there is a thud against the window. You go out to see what it is and come back with a hummingbird cradled in your hands. Its tongue lolls out along your palm, a long hairy forked thing. Its feathers are iridescent green, vibrating with its heartbeat. You tell me to heat sugar water on the stove, and we use a Q-tip to dab the mixture into its mouth. It pulls its tongue in, then rolls it out again, and we dab. Finally, it wakes, scoops one last sip into its beak, hovers mid-air, and with a whirr, disappears out the window.

I am thirteen and you tell me I can bring a friend with me to visit my grandparents' place on Salt Spring Island. I bring Kate, who will only be alive for four more years, but none of us knows that yet, except maybe Kate. She is tall and bold, her hair straight and heavy blonde. Her family are Mennonites or born-again. Some extreme branch of Christianity. All her fingers are double-jointed, and she specializes in making dramatic hand gestures while she speaks. She and I sneak whiskey from my grandparents' liquor cabinet, mix it with orange juice, and drink it out of a water bottle in their backyard. We walk into town smoking cigarettes Kate stole from her older brother's friend. Kate tells me she was raped when she was nine by a group of teenage boys after school, before I knew her. She was walking home alone and they pushed her down behind an empty building at the edge of the schoolyard. I listen like I'm watching a daytime talk show. She passes me the cigarette and I inhale deeply, put my hand on my hip.

Not long after, Kate and I are sitting on the water reservoir in the forest near the university wearing our cutest outfits, sprawled out on the concrete in the sun. She shows me this secret spot, close to her house and miles from mine, surrounded by cedar trees, ferns, and moss. We blow bubbles from a yellow canister with a happy face on it that I wear around my neck. Two years after Kate dies, a woman is murdered near this spot while she's jogging. She's murdered in broad daylight, not far from the reservoir where Kate and I sit. I read about it in the news and I call you. I tell you about Kate and me on the concrete, invincible and free.

I am four and I confide in you that I am so excited to grow up and for you to be the baby so I can rock you in my arms. You spare me the truth, which is perhaps not so different.

I'm twenty-three, hitchhiking across the country, on a highway in the Eastern Townships in Quebec, when I see a russet falcon lying on its back in the road, wings splayed, neck twisted at an ungodly angle. It is breathing and it looks directly at me as I take my backpack off to approach. Its eyes shine yellow and sharp. I gather it in my arms and sit on the shoulder of the highway. I hum Brahms's "Lullaby" as I run a finger down its back. It shudders and exhales its last breath.

I am nineteen, riding my bike to your house, west along the Greenway at dusk. I glance up as a muster of crows swarms east, black silhouettes against a washed-out blue sky.

I stand on a rock in the middle of a lake in the middle of the night. It's slimy with algae. Water up to my waist. I'm with three men I've known since they were boys. We're huddled together in the dark and the moon is a yellow cup in the sky, tilted so Mars spills out, a flickering jewel. We stand close to each other, my pregnant stomach pressed between their bodies. Cool air nips at our shoulders and we dive back in, scramble ashore, lichen between our toes. We stop at the gas station and eat raspberry candy and Ring Pops. Open the doors to our homes. Step over the threshold.

Fourth Floor Looking North

The night I met Julian I had the window down in the car and the radio was pumping. I was wearing the black leather jacket I had bought on layaway at the Bay.

I had been working construction since May, hauling drywall and plastering in the new Science World building the city was putting in for Expo. My body was sore. After work I had to soak, then scrub my hands to get the plaster out of the creases in my knuckles and palms. I had finally saved for my sweet dusty grey Dodge Colt and picked it up that morning. I signed all the papers on the cluttered desk at Lucky Auto, handed over the wad of cash. It was used, the interior smelled like upholstery cleaner, and the clutch was sticky, but it was mine.

On Davie Street the clubs were crawling. People were clustered under blinking neons and lineups stretched the length of the block. It was all tight jeans and moustaches, plumes of cigarette smoke lofting above the queens and queers and punks.

At work I kept quiet. I remember that week after I met Julian, Mark kept asking, "Get any pussy this weekend?"

He was holding a four-by-eight-foot sheet of drywall to studs and insulation, pudgy fingers hyperextending against the pressure, white and bloodless at the tips. Mark had arms like sea cucumbers, hairy and thick. I wanted him to shut up.

"Yeah, sure, " I said, blasting screws along the edge of the drywall. "Was she hot?" he asked.

I jammed on the trigger of the drill. He wanted details, but what was I going to say? I stuffed my earplugs in, lined another drywall screw up with the edge of the sheet.

Outside the club, I turned the music off in the car and lit a cigarette, left the engine running, camouflaged among the taxis and the clamour of Friday night. I rolled the passenger-side window down and waited.

I watched through the windshield as this young guy stumbled out of the bar. He was lanky and tall, his blond hair cut short, with smooth bangs that he flicked off his forehead. His skin was tan and clear, his body graceful and loose as he put a cigarette to his lips, craning toward the security guard, a six-foot-tall drag queen, for a light. He stood on the sidewalk alone, and then he saw me watching him. He came over slowly.

"Can I get a ride?" he asked, bending to the passenger window.

I reached across the seat to unlock the door.

"I'm Julian," he said, easing into the car.

I didn't bring men back to my room at the Patricia Hotel. It was a busy, dank SRO with dark hallways and water-stained walls, cockroaches scuttling in every crack. Even so, I kept my room spic and span. I had a rag rug my mom made me next to the bed and an antique lamp I had picked up at the Sally Ann on the bedside table. But no amount of vinegar could get the goddamn rotten smell out of the buckling linoleum, and I didn't want to screw on my saggy single mattress. Plus, there was no soundproofing between the ten-by-ten rooms and the other tenants would talk.

"Where are we going?" Julian asked.

I didn't respond right away. I watched him rolling up a joint as we drove, caught his delicate collarbone and lean arms, his strong hands deftly working the paper back and forth. He smelled of sweat and cologne.

"Your place?" I asked.

That week there was a lot going on at the Patricia. There had been whisperings of eviction, rumours that the building was going to be bought up and renovated because of Expo. Because they could get more money that way and because we weren't real tenants since it was an SRO. Some university people said the same thing happened before the World's Fair in Knoxville a few years before. My neighbour, May West—"after the dessert, not the actress," she said—was agitated. She had knocked on my door at three a.m. the night before—orange blush caked into her wrinkles, ginger-grey hair wisping out of the bun pinned to the top of her head. Leaned into my room when I cracked the door open, nudged her way over the threshold.

"They'll kill us all," she said, her tone confidential. "That's the plan, did they tell you?"

She jutted her chin up, looked at me appraisingly.

I told her, "No one is killing anyone, and no one knows if the evictions are even happening."

"They'll kill us, all right. First they'll put us out on the street, then they'll pick us off one by one, ship us to the boondocks and feed us to the dogs."

May West had been a ballet dancer, but she liked partying too much to make it big. She laughed when she said this. A low, hoarse growl. She said she was always hungover at rehearsals, then too high to make it at all. She dropped acid with Rudolph Nureyev in New York City in her twenties before she had a passionate romance with Baryshnikov in 1970. She was the real reason he had defected to Canada in 1974. But she had gotten sober by then and was no longer interested, had moved to Vancouver and set up shop in the Patricia.

Julian and I pulled up outside a dilapidated mansion on West 5th and Bayswater. A hipped roof and a pocket window peaked over tall hedges, maroon paint was peeling off wood siding, and the front porch bowed.

There were five roommates in the house, so we had to be quiet. We squeaked up a broad, dusty staircase. Julian's legs were thin and his calves flexed with every step. The soles of his white socks were dark with dirt. He paused on the landing and turned to face me, slipping a hand to my waist.

"My room is all the way at the top," he said. I could smell the booze on his breath, couldn't take my eyes off his lips. I followed him up and up, through dim hallways, past a quarry of books in cardboard boxes, a bike, a smashed acoustic guitar.

Julian's mattress was a double, on the floor. A soft duvet spread neatly, folded down at the top. He lit candles and the room glowed. I felt like my fingers were made of potatoes, like I didn't belong in his world. A bright mandala tapestry covered the wall behind the bed, pinned at two corners and sagging in the middle. A line of string hung across the room with black-and-white photos pinned to it. The city twinkled out the pocket window and Julian's body was warm. I pressed into it, peeled his shirt up and off, held his hips, felt his thighs against my thighs, his stomach against my stomach. I ran my hand up the notches in his spine. When he wrapped his mouth around my dick, I thought the world was melting.

I stayed that night, and the whole next day, and the whole next night. We had sex seven times.

"Eight if you count the time we fell asleep halfway through," Julian said.

We cooked and ate and smoked countless cigarettes in bed and on the deck and in the kitchen. We walked around Julian's bedroom in our underwear, and when our underwear were too dirty to pull on again, we walked around in nothing at all. We showered together and had sex in the shower. Julian took photos of me lying naked on the bed. I propped myself up on my elbow and stared into the lens.

"Lick your lips," said Julian. "It makes them look better on film." I licked my lips and Julian clicked the shutter, wound the film, and clicked it again.

When it was time for me to get back to my place on Sunday night I borrowed a change of clothes. After work the next day, I washed them and dried them, folded them into a neat stack—jeans, T-shirt, underwear, socks. I was so sure it would be more than just a one-time thing, so sure it would be important.

A month later Julian still hadn't called and we were all evicted from the Patricia with a day's notice. The renovations started right away and I heard they rented those rooms out for over $100 a night. But I had enough money to get into a good spot on Pender, an apartment in a big co-op with a fresh coat of paint and new floors. I boxed up my stuff and drove the two blocks to my new place. I put Julian's clothes carefully on top of my own, unpacked them first, and kept them on a chair in my bedroom. In all fairness, I hadn't called him either.

May West ended up at Bill Hennessey, an apartment block just down the street, across from a corner store with a huge sign in the front window that said, "U2" in big red letters, and then "Grocery" in small letters next to it. For some reason, I never read that sign as a reference to the band but as some bold effort to include everyone on the block in the store's dingy shopping experience. May West was on the fourth floor looking north toward the mountains, and everyone said, "Isn't it so nice and clean?" But she hated it.

"Who wants pink carpets?" she said. "Who wants melamine cupboards?"

Bill Hennessey was brand new, a big stucco cube of social housing, and it still smelled like plastic and the chemicals from new flooring. May West took to her bed the first week after the move. She didn't leave it except to go to the bathroom and to eat a few bites here and there. She lost weight and stopped wearing makeup or doing her hair. Her pink nightie turned grey and the smell off her was vile, even she knew it. Her white roots came in and the back of her hair was matted from lying down. The apartment was stuffy. She kept the lights off and the curtains drawn. The only food in the fridge was stuff I brought.

"Oh, no dear, I couldn't eat with my stomach in a knot like this," she said. "The stink of those carpets is just too much. Those chemicals cause cancer, you know."

"Maybe we should open a window," I said.

But if it wasn't the light, it was the breeze or the smell or the sound or something awful that wasn't how it should be, that wasn't how it had been at the Patricia Hotel. No amount of coaxing and cajoling could bring May West back to herself.

Expo started shortly after we moved. The construction company I worked for had a new contract at an office building on Alberni, and on my first day off I walked down to the fair to pick up two tickets to see Baryshnikov. A gift for May West. I thought I might try to get her backstage after the show, lift her spirits. When I got down to Science World the crowds were thick. A clown with peppery black hair and big shoes was folding himself into a barrel, feet on either side of his head, flexed to the sky. An entourage of black limousines with little flags waving on the hood was parked in a line, and I heard someone say it was Prince Charles and Lady Di. And then I saw her.

Princess Diana was delicate like a moth. Her dress had pleats around the waist and her nylons were translucent white. She was wearing shiny white kitten heels with pointed toes like garden spades. A long double row of pearls looped tight around her neck, drooped low over crisp white taffeta. A shiny white half-moon purse hung from her shoulder on a long string. Her hair poofed and swooped, and her earlobes peeked out, covered by big pearl earrings. She paused at all the right angles for photos.

I watched her move slowly toward the California Pavilion, flanked by her husband and a sea of stiff men in navy blue and black, some government officials, some military, and then a flock of press. Under all the makeup and silk, she must have been exhausted. But she nodded and smiled, tilted her head attentively, and they all buoyed her along. There was something about her slender neck and her calves that reminded me of Julian. Pale and innocent.

I walked into the California Pavilion behind the paparazzi and Diana fans, then up a flight of stairs. I leaned against a railing, watched her float along as people pushed past me. She wasn't more than twenty feet away, walking toward a group of children in wheelchairs and on crutches, assembled behind a rope. She bent down and shook hands with each of them, her purse swinging forward and her hair swooshing with it. When she straightened up, her shoulders hunched for just a few seconds too long.

She was ushered toward three computer monitors with a banner above them that read, "Design Your Own Bicycle." A man in a suit was explaining the exhibit to her, showing her how she could make a custom bike, choose the colour and the seat and the shape of the handlebars. I imagined Lady Di on a bike. Her pencil skirt hiked up around her hips, hair blowing in the wind.

Then there was a commotion. Someone shoved into my back and I pitched forward. The rail dug into my stomach and I felt the perforated ticket stubs tear against my body. As I reached into my jacket pocket to pull them out, smoothing the crease, flattening the tear, there was a shout from below. A swarm of men rushed toward the computer monitors. The paparazzi pressed in, cameras flashing, and as the crowd cleared I saw Diana, shimmering and white, on the floor. There was this holy stillness under the high ceilings, then someone yelled.

"Get a doctor! She fainted."

As the cameras flashed, I looked just off to the left and there was Julian, with his thighs against the rope that cordoned Lady Di off from the rest of us. He was straining against it, his camera held up to his face, the crowd jostling against him. I thought then of lying on his bed, of his eyes looking at me over the camera, of him telling me to lick my lips, and of how I would have done anything he asked. Would still. I called out to him, but the noise had picked up again and he didn't hear me over the din, and then over the sirens. By the time I elbowed my way down the stairs, I couldn't find him in the crowd.

When I got back to May West's apartment that evening with the Baryshnikov tickets, an ambulance was there. Someone had reported the smell from her apartment to the building manager, claimed they thought she had died. There was talk of her being admitted to Riverview. When the police arrived, she was perched on the concrete railing of her balcony, clutching an iron, smoothing the air like a mime, her filthy nightie flapping around her ankles as she screamed obscenities into the afternoon.

Warmer Soon

I was having a bad winter. They were going to fire me from the restaurant for sleeping through a staff meeting and eating day-olds that were garbage anyway, so I quit. They had started asking us to save the prosciutto when we threw out the old sandwiches, dab off any remnants of pesto or arugula, and wrap the meat in aluminum foil to be reused. The veggie sandwiches went straight in the trash, though, so honestly, what difference did it make if I took those home? Plus I couldn't afford to keep the apartment as hot as my roommate wanted it. He blasted the baseboard heater in his room and I snuck in after he left for class or work to turn it off. I squeezed my arm down next to his bed until I felt the ridges of the dial grip against my fingertips, clicked it all the way to the left. Sometimes I forgot to turn it back on before he got home and I hoped he didn't notice. My room was so cold I had to wear a sweater and a toque to bed. It was one of those rooms in between two rooms that doesn't have a window to the outside. My window was frosted glass and through it were the obscured shadows of the kitchen. There was zero airflow. The wall in my closet wasn't insulated and condensation from the cold outside had caused mould to penetrate eight hangers' worth of clothes. They were all covered in a thick green fuzz. I asked my landlord to buy a dehumidifier and he told me to turn the heat up.

My apartment was on the top floor of a duplex and it was compact. The stackable washer and dryer were pressed up against the dining table. It had a door that was supposed to lead to the back deck, but there was no deck. Instead, it opened to a twenty-foot drop into the back alley. I had nightmares about accidentally walking out that door. I also dreamt repeatedly about finding other rooms in the apartment that I didn't know existed and made it much more spacious and livable. In the dreams, I would crawl through a secret door behind my dresser, like the door in *Being John Malkovich*. Instead of finding myself in a brain, there I was in a luxurious sitting room with a purple velvet chaise longue, tasselled drapery, and a floral-print rug in front of a crackling fireplace.

It had reached that point in winter where my nose hairs froze when I went outside and took a deep breath, but I didn't have a winter coat. Just a raincoat that I would layer sweaters under and a wool coat that I bought at the friperie. I dried it on hot and washed it and dried it again to get rid of the smell of the thrift store, bedbugs, dust mites, old skin cells. I was very cold all the time. I layered wool tights under my jeans. I was perpetually hungry from the cold.

My grandmother had moved from Saint-Lambert into an old folks' building in the north island. Her old place had a veranda where she kept lush basil and tomatoes, hanging planters brimming with begonias, fuchsia, and geraniums. She had a white glider chair and footrest on the veranda. When I was a kid she would make us green tea. She sat on the chair and I sat on the footrest and we glided there together, breathing in the humidity and the smell of the herbs and flowers as the sun went down, glinting off the gold windows of the Casino de Montréal on the other side of the highway. Her building had a rooftop pool I loved. I went swimming late at night and my grandma sat on the turf deck of the pool, glamorous on a sun chair in her robe and slippers, smoking. I could see her bunions in those slippers. She had long, lean legs that she liked to show off, and she let one slip out through the slit of her robe. We watched the fireworks explode over La Ronde from the pool as my lips turned blue. The new place in the north island had horseshoes on the lawn by the river, monthly birthday parties for the residents, and an aviary. My grandmother was angry all the time and had started having paranoid delusions.

I took the bus to visit her every second weekend. It was a long ride. In mid-January, I was on my way out to see her when I ran into the mailman. He handed me a letter and the return address said it was from my best friend back home, Lucy. I saved it for the bus. Since I'd left, Lucy and I only communicated through letters. Lucy said texting and email felt meaningless and she was too awkward on the phone. I was sitting in those seats that are a group of four, two facing forward and two facing toward them, and two teenage boys were sitting across from me. Our knees were playing Tetris. The boys stared at their phones, showing each other YouTube videos and laughing. The smell of cheap cologne wafted off them.

In the letter, Lucy told me how much she missed me. She told me that she had broken up with her boyfriend a couple of weeks before. She told me that just after they broke up she found out she was pregnant. That at first she was in shock, and then she started to dream about the baby. She bought leopard-print maternity leggings, even though her body hadn't changed size. She drew the plans for a DIY side sleeper to attach to her bed. She told me that she was almost three months into the pregnancy, and that she had just had a miscarriage the day before she wrote the letter. That's why she was writing. To tell me how terrible it was. To still feel nauseous, to still feel pregnant, but to know that it was gone. She told me that she had passed a clot like a boiled beet. Plop. That she wished I were there and could come over, make her tea, and lie in bed with her and hold her. That she felt so alone. I started to weep on the bus and the ink from her letter ran down the page onto my fingers. The boys in the seats facing me went silent and looked at me and then looked at their phones, but I couldn't stop weeping.

When I got off the bus it was dark and freezing. I called my mom as I walked down Boulevard Gouin, glancing over my shoulder occasionally at the empty street behind me. I told her how terrible everything was, how cold I was, and how Lucy was so sad and so far away. I told my mom I missed her, and I missed Lucy. She said she wanted to hug me, and it was killing her that she couldn't just reach through the phone and make everything okay. I held the phone away from my ear and closed my eyes. I pointed the speaker at my cheek while my mom spoke. The sound waves sent soft puffs of air from the speaker onto my face and I pretended they were my mom's breath.

She said she would e-transfer me money to buy a proper winter coat. I said she didn't have to, but she insisted. I started weeping again, partly because I was so cold and partly because I knew I would be warmer soon.

I signed my name in the logbook at the concierge's desk. My grandmother opened her apartment door and told me that I was late. The food was on the table. She had roasted a chicken and made tomato aspic. I told her I was having a bad day and she said she was, too. She told me all about how she had done two hours of laundry and dusted the whole apartment. She switched from English to French, and back again, without even noticing she was doing it. She told me that she had spent three hours in the kitchen making supper. She told me she thought the building staff had come into her apartment while she was sleeping and switched the doorknobs to handles.

"They used to be knobs," she said, as she showed me the bathroom door. "Now they're handles," she said. She pushed down on the handle, opened the door, and then closed it, as if the motions were evidence.

When I got home my roommate was still out. I crept into his room and turned his heater back on. That night I dreamt about the small door behind my dresser. This time it had a door handle like the ones in my grandmother's apartment. I pushed down on the handle and the door swung into a palatial room I had not known about. All the extra space was such a relief. The room had high ceilings with ornate mouldings and plasterwork. A cut crystal chandelier hung in the centre. My grandmother was there, young and ethereal as she put my hair in rag curlers. She was wearing her silk robe and her slippers and she smelled like jasmine. In the morning, I woke to my phone buzzing on my bedside table. It was my grandmother. She wanted to know if I had stolen two side plates from her apartment.

"No, Grandma," I said. "You know I would never steal from you."

As I said it I felt a pang of guilt for stealing brie from the deli of the fancy grocery store on Saint-Viateur. Greek yogourt on Park, the coconut flavour. A pair of wax earplugs from the Jean Coutu. I missed the sensor on the box of earplugs and the alarm went off as I was exiting. I knew I had passed the security guard up an aisle by the pharmacy, so I just kept walking. The two cashiers came running out onto the sidewalk in their red smocks. Short middle-aged women, imploring me to come back in so they could take my picture. I turned to face them and felt my palms sweating, my heart heavy.

"I don't know what you're talking about," I said, and walked away quickly.

My grandmother would have been so ashamed if she knew. It would have confirmed all her suspicions.

The year before I left Vancouver, Lucy and I smoked a lot of weed, ate mushrooms, and drank rosé on my porch, watching the sun set. I got so stoned I thought I was dying. My whole body and brain went numb. We would go for long bike rides together in the rain. One time, after smoking up, we were sitting in a bar on Main Street and I whispered in Lucy's ear that I couldn't feel my limbs, and I thought I might forget how to breathe. She said she felt like she was watching herself from outside her body. She took my hand between hers and rubbed so I could feel it. Her hands were cool and dry. They swished as she rubbed. We walked back to her apartment holding hands, my head spinning, Lucy bracing me against the world. She made me peanut butter toast and we lay in her bed staring at the ceiling, talking about death, until the weed wore off. She wrapped her body around me, and we slept like that.

On Halloween, I drank too many pomegranate cocktails and ate too many weed brownies. I barfed so much that Lucy called the paramedics. My legs felt like giant slugs pulsating on the tile floor. I was hyperventilating, and I hugged the cold ceramic toilet bowl just to feel grounded.

"If I die, tell my mom I love her," I said.

When the paramedics came, they said I could go to the hospital, or I could just wait it out in the bathroom until my stomach was empty and the weed wore off. They all stayed with me, Lucy and the two paramedics, while I barfed and barfed and barfed. When I finally stopped, the paramedics left and I asked Lucy to call my mom. I was too old to be calling my mom for a ride after a bad trip, but I did it anyway.

Just before I moved to Montreal, Lucy and I smoked a joint at Wreck Beach. We were picking blackberries, eating them and saving some in yogourt containers to bring home. It was hot and we were caked in salt and sand, our freckles popping off our faces. I took a blackberry and squished it between my fingers, leaned into Lucy and told her to hold still. I slid the smashed berry down the centre of her forehead and along the bridge of her nose. I kept sliding the berry down her chin, down her throat, between her breasts to her belly button, and down to her crotch. I slid my finger down over her pubic bone, and then stepped back to inspect my work. She laughed and her shoulders came up around her ears. She laughed so hard her boobs jiggled, and she took a handful of berries and crushed them. She smeared the juice on my cheeks, and then my stomach, my shoulders, my thighs. We giggled, then we went serious, and Lucy took photos of us on her film camera. We rinsed it all off in the ocean.

When Lucy got those photographs developed, we flipped through them together in her kitchen, admiring the bruises of blackberry juice all over our naked bodies. Ridiculous sombre expressions on our faces. She gave me a picture of her standing with her back to the ocean, looking straight into the camera. Her skin is tanned gold and her hair is long and wavy, bleached copper from the sun. She has one hand shielding her eyes and a purple line running down her middle. Her mouth is open, like she's in the middle of saying something, and she has a splotch of purple on the right side of her upper lip. With her other hand, she's holding a container full of blackberries, gesturing toward the water. I love her in that photo. I love her.

I didn't call Lucy right after receiving her letter. I knew she hated talking on the phone, or maybe I wished she had just called me in the first place. I guess I felt like a letter should be replied to with a letter. But then I didn't have time to write to her, or maybe I didn't want to. I went to Jeans Jeans Jeans and bought a down-filled parka.

"Better than Canada Goose," the salesman told me. I spent every penny of the $300 my mom had sent.

At home, I pulled the photo of Lucy with the blackberry smears out of an old notebook and slipped it in the frame of my mirror with her letter just below. I stood there in my parka, looking in the mirror and looking at Lucy.

Almost Touching

Bailey sits in the back seat because there are no airbags in the powder-blue Chevy Nova. The ripped vinyl upholstery digs into her thighs, and she pulls at the yellow foam disintegrating out of the tear. Joy turns down the driveway into the underground parkade, headlights casting a quick glow over the dark corners like the searchlight from Playland that scans the city on summer nights.

The johns park in the visitors' lot for their blow jobs and Bailey likes to catch their nervous glances out side-view mirrors or rear windshields. Sometimes there are no cars, just one person huddled in the corner, the contents of her purse spilled out in front of her. Tonight, there is a fancy car, shiny and black. It's early evening and the sky is pink to purple to blue. Bailey cranes to see through the windows of the parked car.

"What's she doing?" Bailey asks.

"She's a hooker," says Joy.

"What's he doing?"

"He's a john."

These are the words they use in the neighbourhood, but they are not really answers. Bailey's uncle's name is John and she finds this worrisome. John lives with her other uncle, Julian, and at supper that evening, Bailey asks which one of them will wear the wedding dress when they get married. John says marriage is an institution that has rejected gay people and they don't want to be part of it. When Bailey asks what an institution is, they give other examples like schools or the church or the government, and Bailey imagines marriage as a big grey building with lots of offices.

John and Julian live in the same co-op as Bailey and her mom, just across the courtyard. When Julian moved in with John, they did a fancy paint job on the walls in their living room with sponges and rich yellow paint and hung framed prints of Julian's black-and-white photography. They hung a portrait of Grace Jones next to the dining room table and put dimmer switches on all the lights that mattered. Bailey likes how shiny Grace Jones's lips are in that portrait, and she likes the cigarette hanging out of the corner of her mouth. She thinks Grace Jones is like a boy, but with boobs, and she likes that, too.

The complex has 200 suites, with laneways leading to each row of suites, and it has an apartment building with 100 apartments. Some of it is social housing, some of it is subsidized, and some of it is privately owned. All the suites are connected, so when one house gets mice, the whole row gets mice and extermination is very complicated. Over the past winter, Joy and Bailey discovered a nest of mice in their couch. The mother was nowhere to be found, but a clutch of pink pups was wriggling around blind in the batting of one of the cushions. When the exterminator came Bailey cried as he placed the mice in a box, held on to her mom's waist, and buried her face in Joy's soft stomach. The exterminator found a colony under the floor in the crawl space. Hundreds of mice, he said, burrows and tunnels running the whole length of their row. Luckily, there are no cockroaches, which is a relief because their scuttle makes Bailey sick. When the exterminator was investigating the extent of the mouse infestation he knocked a hole in the back wall of Bailey and Joy's unit. In one spot the hammer accidentally went all the way through the drywall on the other side. Bailey peered over the exterminator's shoulder, and in the gleam of light shining through the hole, she saw right into Kevin Paul's living room. When she thinks of this now, Bailey likes to imagine what it would be like if the co-op had no walls, everyone living there in their houses almost touching. Couches back to back, spines curved against each other.

There are tall stands of bamboo growing in cedar planters in front of every suite in the complex, and all the laneways connect to a big walkway down the centre that is brick in some parts, with moss growing in the cracks that Bailey and her best friend Ruby-Lynn like to pick out with sticks. There is a circular playground with monkey bars and grass, and there is a laundry room across from it that wafts out the smell of dryer as tenants come and go with laundry baskets. There is rose campion planted all over, the type with bright pink flowers, and there are these tall thin trees that have no branches or leaves on their trunks but a great canopy overhead. They don't grow like that but are pruned that way so there are not as many places for people to hide to shoot up, or smoke crack, or have sex. The rhododendron bushes are kept bushy, though, and Bailey often finds discarded syringes in the cedar mulch that covers the soil.

It's Friday and Bailey will be spending the evening at Ruby-Lynn's house. Joy is going out. Her long brown hair is still wet from the bath, and she's sitting in front of her vanity table in nylons and a bra. That soft bit of flesh between the two spills over the elastic waistband. Bailey pushes on that bit of fat, and then wraps her arms around it, tries to mush her body right into her mom's, tries to get their hearts to touch. Bailey thinks her mom is the most beautiful person she has ever seen, sliding lipstick over her soft lips, the corners of her mouth pulled back so they are firm against her teeth. The shade is called Crimson Kiss.

While her mom blow-dries her hair, Bailey watches the women working across Pender Street through the gaps in the venetian blinds. It's dusk and their silhouetted shapes move slowly up past the Chinese community centre. One woman stoops to pick up a cigarette butt, the other digging around in the shiny green leaves of the periwinkle that lines the complex, searching for something. This is before dime bags, when drugs are wrapped in tidy sections cut out of black garbage bags and tied up into bundles, like a miniature traveller might attach to the end of a stick and carry over their shoulder. People in the neighbourhood are forever searching in the periwinkle, as though there is a secret lottery, a chance of coming across a stash in a bush, treasure at the foot of a tree, the possibility of finding some discarded remnant of something worth keeping, something good.

When her mom comes in the living room, Bailey is drawing the outfits she would wear if she were working with the women on the street.

"This one's got a purple miniskirt with black platforms. And she got this purse for Christmas from her sister," says Bailey, holding up the picture.

"Why is she so dressed up?"

"She's going off to work."

Bailey knows there is sex involved in that work because Ruby-Lynn's mom, Yvonne, is a hooker, and Ruby-Lynn tells Bailey all kinds of stories about how her mom has to lick men down there. Bailey imagines licking Joseph down there, and she thinks that would be very unpleasant. She saw his balls once in class when he had a hole in the crotch of his pants and sat on the floor with his knees tucked into his chest. They were all veiny.

Joy doesn't like it when the women work right in front of the complex because it means their pimps and dealers are there, too. Bailey is scared of the men on the block. Some have neck tattoos, and they all have this walk like their knees are made of Jell-O and might not keep them upright. They swear and scan the ground and the bushes. But she loves watching the women because they are so glamorous in their high heels and short skirts. She hopes she will be that sexy when she grows up. She practises standing the way they stand, one foot crossed in front of the other, a purse on her shoulder. She leans forward, pretending to talk through a car window, or squirming in that way people squirm in the neighbourhood. She sticks her thumb out and puts on her mom's lipstick, which she borrows in secret from the drawer in her vanity, next to a stout bottle of Dior perfume. When she walks, she stands on her tiptoes and sways her hips from side to side with each step. Bailey loves the texture of her white cotton tummy top. It's rough and has flowers woven into the cotton with tiny holes in their centres where she can see the pink of her skin. She rubs her finger in circles over those pulses of flesh. Then she climbs on the bunk bed and jumps off into a pile of blankets. She holds an open umbrella while she jumps and she is sure she's flying.

"How do I look?" asks Joy. Her hair is loose around her shoulders and she has on a blue, long-sleeved blouse, a black pencil skirt, and a silk scarf with rows of multicoloured sparkles running through it.

"Like a million bucks," says Bailey, as she runs her hands through the ends of her mom's silky hair.

Ruby-Lynn lives with her dad, Murray, in a ground-level apartment. It's dimly lit, with worn brown carpets, and smells like stale cigarette smoke and dollar store shampoo. When Bailey gets there, she and Ruby-Lynn go into Ruby-Lynn's bedroom and block the door with a big Rubbermaid container of toys. They turn tricks with Ruby-Lynn's teddy bears, which involves hugging and kissing them and telling them how much they love them. Ruby-Lynn puts a stuffed animal down her pants and moves her hips in big circles. She picks up a Ken doll and swings around to Bailey.

"If he unzips his fly, you have to kiss him under his underwear," she says, holding the doll up to Bailey's face, pants around his ankles. Bailey gives his smooth plastic crotch a peck.

Murray is dozing with a beer in front of the TV when they flop down on the couch and Ruby-Lynn flicks through the channels to *Sweet Valley High*. He heaves himself up and to the kitchen.

"I'm making spaghetti," he says. "And when it's ready, it's tube off."

Bailey nods vigorously, eyes glued to the TV as she dips a baby carrot into the bowl of ketchup Ruby-Lynn has provided. Ruby-Lynn dips everything in ketchup. On the TV the twins, Jess and Liz, are wearing matching leopard-print bikinis.

Bailey and Ruby-Lynn have known each other since Bailey was born, two months after Ruby-Lynn. In the photos in their parents' albums, their moms are exhausted as they sit around on living room floors or park benches, wide-eyed babies between them. That was before Yvonne started using again and Murray got custody.

Bailey and Ruby-Lynn are the only white girls in the complex, and the Chinese kids call them lo fan. At school, Connie told Bailey that lo fan means "white ghost," in Cantonese, or maybe "white devil," and is definitely an insult. Connie has greasy, long hair and covers her mouth when she speaks. Her skin is smooth like porcelain and she has this one tooth that comes out of the roof of her mouth behind her other teeth. Bailey thinks it makes her look like Drusilla on *Buffy the Vampire Slayer* and wonders if that tooth helps with chewing.

Connie, Bailey, and Ruby-Lynn play Chinese skip rope at recess and lunch most days, and Bailey thinks Connie must be really mature because she wears a bra and keeps sanitary pads in her desk. Bailey's mom told her that when the kids in the complex call her lo fan she can tell them it's mean, but she isn't allowed to use the racist words the other white kids use at school. Bailey promised her mom she wouldn't, but she tried out the words anyway to see what would happen. The first time she felt a rush. The second time she felt guilty. The third time, as she watched Gary's face fall, she felt terrible.

At the dinner table Ruby-Lynn skips the spaghetti sauce and squirts ketchup all over her noodles. She asks Murray when Yvonne is going to come visit. Murray says he doesn't know, and then he finishes his beer.

"She's gone AWOL, Ruby-Lynn, AWOL."

Ruby-Lynn nods and sucks a noodle into her mouth. Bailey watches it slither up off her plate.

When Joy comes to pick Bailey up, Ruby-Lynn answers the door. Murray is passed out on the couch with the TV blasting the news. Bailey stuffs her shoes on and slips her hand into her mom's.

In the morning, when the sky is still pink with the sunrise, the grannies do tai chi in the complex courtyard. Bailey likes how slowly they move, and she tries to move with that degree of control. It's mid-September, the last of the warm days. When she gets to the playground, Ruby-Lynn is waiting for her with a dinky water gun. André sees them and comes running, holding a dead mouse by the tail. He's four years older than them, and he wears baggy pants and a backward baseball cap.

"Found something for you, Bailey," André says, wagging the mouse back and forth.

After they bury the mouse and recite the funeral rites, André gets his Super Soaker and Bailey hooks the hose up to the tap outside the door leading down to the parkade. When André starts pumping his water gun, Ruby-Lynn takes off. Instead of following her, André turns to Bailey. He fires at her chest and she lets the hose rip, thumb over the open nozzle to get it blasting, and soaks his crotch.

"You peed your pants!" she shrieks.

He runs toward her and drops the Super Soaker. He grabs the hose from her and throws it to the ground, then shoves Bailey against the wall. Over his shoulder she watches the water from the hose spill down the centre of the complex, a cool black stream on grey concrete. Then she feels the sharp smack of the stucco digging into her shoulder blades. André pushes his knee into Bailey's crotch and thrusts his hands under her shirt, pinching her nipples between his thumbs and index fingers. She gasps with the pain. Her breasts are only the size of cherry pits, but the nubs under her skin are painful. She stomps on his foot, tries to shake him off. André is strong. When she finally wriggles free she whips around and gets down into a lunge. She starts moving really slowly, with her hands spread flat and her fingers together, like the grannies doing tai chi.

"Freak," says André, and he shoves her into the stucco again, but before he can get back under her shirt, she kicks him and ducks away, sprinting in the direction of Ruby-Lynn. Bailey's gaining distance when she looks back and stumbles on a crack in the brick path. She goes down hard on her side and when she lands she feels a spike in her leg, then a sharp crack under her weight as she breaks the fall with her elbow.

"Ruby-Lynn!" She's yelling. "Ruby-Lynn!"

When Ruby-Lynn reaches her, Bailey is clutching her thigh. André hangs back. Ruby-Lynn crouches beside her and slowly peels Bailey's hands from her leg. She leans in close. Bailey can feel her breath on her skin, can smell her shampoo. For a moment she doesn't feel pain, and then her skin starts to sting.

"What is it?" Ruby-Lynn asks.

Bailey's thigh is scraped where she fell, and there is a red dot in the centre of the raw patch. As they examine it, she feels it throb. The orange cap of a needle is on the ground, and when Bailey bends her knee up the clear part of the syringe and the orange plunger are under her. Bailey let's Ruby-Lynn run her index finger over the red spot, and she feels Ruby-Lynn's fingertip catch on something sharp and hard in the middle.

On December 23 the co-op holds its annual Christmas party. Bailey and Joy go as a matter of tradition, and Bailey is excited for the gift she'll receive under the synthetic tree. As usual, the complex caretaker, Antonio, is Santa. Stuffed stomach and a terrible matted beard. The party is a potluck, and Joy has made a quiche. She is wearing a black miniskirt with gold lamé flowers on it, translucent black nylons, and a sheer black tank top with a black velvet bolero overtop. Bailey can see her mom's bra through the tank top, and she thinks the outline of her cleavage is so sexy. She pulls her shirt down to see if she has any cleavage, but it's all flat.

Inside is loud with kids shrieking and festive chatter. A long table is covered in a mix of traditional Christmas food and Chinese food—a roast turkey next to stir-fried gai lan, mashed potatoes, and a heaping platter of chow mein. Older residents are sitting at the round tables decorated with red polyester tablecloths. The centrepieces are artificial holly wreaths around battery-powered candles. Plastic flames flicker everywhere.

Bailey sees Ruby-Lynn across the room. She's sitting next to the Christmas tree. Bailey cranes to see who she's talking to and there is André, bending an ear into Ruby-Lynn's hand cupped around her mouth. Ruby-Lynn lets her hand rest on André's shoulder for a second, then tucks her hair behind her ear. André doesn't look at Ruby-Lynn but turns and spots Bailey watching them. He laughs raucously then, as though Ruby-Lynn has said something really funny, but Ruby-Lynn sees Bailey, too. She pushes up from her chair and rushes over. They've barely seen each other since Bailey fell on the needle. They're in different classes and Bailey stopped playing in the complex playground after that day. She's been going home for lunch and walking straight home after school, checking around corners and over her shoulder for André, careful where she's stepping. Ruby-Lynn gives Bailey a hug, then Bailey lifts her skirt to show her the spot on her thigh where they had to cut in to make sure they got the whole tip of the syringe out. Bailey was in the hospital for two days, then had to take a month's worth of antiretroviral medication that made her so sick she couldn't get out of bed.

"You can't really see it," she says, taking Ruby-Lynn's finger and running it over the bump under her tights. "Three stitches," she says.

The scar feels like a hard line of thread.

"André and I are playing flashlight tag after dinner," says Ruby-Lynn.

"What about your gift?"

"André says the gifts are stupid."

Bailey piles a plate with food. Egg foo yong, turkey, spiced yam, and some quiche so her mom doesn't feel bad. She pours gravy over the whole plate and sits down with Ruby-Lynn at an empty table close to the Christmas tree.

"Isn't André cute?" asks Ruby-Lynn.

Bailey hasn't told her about how André shoved her against the wall, about the stucco against her shoulder blades, about the hard pinch, the thrust of his knee in her crotch, the feel of his hands on her skin. She takes a bite of quiche and doesn't answer.

As they finish their food the music stops. There's the sound of bells and Antonio comes into the hall, letting out a deep "Ho ho ho." The kids stop in their tracks and the smallest ones rush over. Bailey sees André heading for the door to the courtyard and Ruby-Lynn jumps up from the table.

"I'm going to go play flashlight tag," she says.

Bailey turns back to Antonio and her mom is standing next to him, gripping a glass of wine. He has a sack of presents slung over one shoulder and he lets out another laugh. As he turns toward the kids, Bailey sees him reach his free hand around Joy's back and stroke her ass. Joy pulls her bolero over her chest with her spare hand as she searches the room for Bailey. Bailey turns away, eyes on her plate, shifting her quiche through a pool of gravy.

Antonio sits next to the tree and fishes around in his sack of gifts. Bailey walks over to her mom. Joy has a thin stain of wine wrapping around the inside edge of her lips and her cheeks are flushed. Antonio pulls out a big box and calls Bailey's name. It's bath stuff from the Body Shop, satsuma scented, her favourite. Body wash, soap, moisturizer, and an orange loofah. After she opens it, Joy insists that she go and sit on Antonio's lap for a picture.

"Mom, that's embarrassing," Bailey says.

"This might be your last year getting anything."

Bailey tugs down the hem of her skirt as she sits on Antonio's lap. She feels him lay his hand on her side, just before the flash goes. Bailey gets up quickly and squeezes away from the other kids crowding around the tree and out the door to the courtyard. The cold night washes over her.

Outside is quiet and the sky is dark. There is no sign of Ruby-Lynn and André. The wind nips through Bailey's tights. She is not allowed out alone at night, and the thrill of it thrums in her stomach. She wanders up the brick walkway toward the centre of the complex. She hears her mom come out from the rec room behind her, hears the door slam as she peers down the first laneway. She hears her mom call her name as she gets farther and farther from the party. The light above the laundry room door flickers yellow and a moth bounces off the glass fixture. Bailey turns down the lane just past the laundry room, the lane on the way to André's house. There are no street lights in the laneways and she is engulfed in darkness. Her mom yells again, but this time Bailey can barely hear her. Her voice is faint and far. Bailey's eyes are searching for something to focus on, and then she sees movement. She can just make out André's silhouette at the end of the lane as he turns, starts coming toward her.

"Where's Ruby-Lynn?" she says, loud enough so he can hear, but he doesn't answer.

She suddenly regrets leaving the party, regrets not answering her mom's call. Her breathing is fast and shallow. She stops walking as André gets closer. André is five houses away and she still can't see his face. He has his hoodie pulled up over his hat and it's all shadowy. Bailey asks again where Ruby-Lynn is and he picks up his pace. She backs up a few steps, but he keeps coming toward her. She turns and starts to run back the way she came, hears his feet beating after her. She won't make it back to the party, she thinks, she's not fast enough. She reels around the corner out of the laneway, past the laundry room, then barrels down the centre walkway, her legs whipping through the night. She watches the ground, determined not to trip this time. Bailey turns to look over her shoulder and André is right behind her, reaching out. Her lungs are burning. She feels herself begin to fall. But there is her mom rushing toward her, Ruby-Lynn following. And Joy pulls her up. Bailey feels the gold lamé of her mom's skirt catching on her tights. Her arms are around her mom's neck, her legs wrapped around her waist.

"I'm here," says Joy, holding Bailey so there's no air between them, so their bodies are seamless. Bailey can feel their hearts pounding against each other, her own slowing to match her mom's. They're syncopated, and then they're the same. She breathes in Joy's perfume and feels the cold wind drying the tears on her cheeks.

Float

I think the float will be an enlightenment. I think the weight-
lessness, the confinement, the disorientation will transport me to a
new plane. That it will take me back to the womb. That it will be a
rebirth. That the deprivation of my senses will release me from their
bondage. I think it will inspire me, that I will emerge unstoppable,
my creative force unleashed. I buy the spa package as a birthday
present for myself. I reserve an afternoon appointment a week in
advance. I wake on my birthday morning full of hope for the day and
the year ahead. I hear a truck idling outside my front door and voices
conferring loudly. When I poke my head out, I see two men removing
a dead cat from my front step.

"He must have been hit," the city worker says, as he holds a black
garbage bag open and the other man lowers the carcass slowly to the
bottom. There is a pool of blood on the concrete.

I have just returned home, alone again, moved my few boxes from
storage. I met the boyfriend I have just left on a cruise ship. He was

working and I was on a budget Mediterranean package I lucked into on points. He had long hair that was bleached by the sun. I kissed him in the galley, after hours. We had sex for the first time just moments later. I lifted one thigh onto the deep-freeze, hiked my skirt up, and leaned back on my hands as he gripped my butt cheeks and fumbled into me. Instead of boarding my flight home from Gibraltar, I got on his flight to Marseille, and when we arrived in the very early morning we walked into his childhood bedroom hand in hand. A faded navy and maroon plaid quilt, a poster on the wall with a French flag and a footballer mid-kick that said "Zizou" in bubbly letters over his head. He kept the room in his mother's home because, he said, it didn't make sense to find a place for those few months a year that he wasn't on a ship. We slept tightly spooned in his single bed that night and every night after that. By morning the sheets were soaked in sweat.

On the second day, his mother showed me her mastectomy scar and I thought of the goddess Diana. The surgery and reconstruction had been done over twenty years before, and her nipple was tattooed back on in a dark brown spiral, like a lollipop at a fun fair. Her neon green budgie was perched on her shoulder. When people think of Diana, they think of the statue of the Roman goddess, *Diana with a Doe*, a masculine huntress reaching into the quiver on her back for an arrow. But the Ephesian counterpart has rows and rows of teats covering her whole torso and orphaned animals suckling off them, though some people have said they aren't breasts but bull testicles. She is the goddess of wild beasts and fertility. Paradoxically, she is also an eternal virgin. Maybe it was the budgie on his mother's shoulder that made me think of Diana, or maybe it was the nonchalance of the exhibition. When she showed me the reconstructed breast it was perfunctory. I didn't ask to see, she just volunteered it. An explanation for why she no longer went topless at the beach, which was where we were headed that morning, towels over our shoulders, beach bags stuffed with supplies for the day. She held a can of aerosol surface cleaner in one hand for her morning chores, had a cigarette stuck to her lips, and pulled out one of her earbuds for the conversation. She was wearing a tank top over a black underwire bra and lifted both layers on one side to show me. I could hear the Bee Gees buzzing out from the tiny speaker dangling by her collarbone.

His mother made coffee cake for breakfast, the top dusted with granulated sugar and cinnamon. She had it on the table with a jug of orange juice. Our plates were laid out with cutlery, glasses, and paper napkins. Once we were settled at the table, she put her earbuds back in. As we ate, the budgie watched us from his perch on her shoulder while she spritzed and polished the shelves in the living room, taking down each ceramic knick-knack and spritzing and polishing those, too. She sang "I Started a Joke" quietly to herself, her cigarette bouncing between her lips. We sipped our juice.

Some days later we took a trip to Paris. I had always wanted to go and I found twenty-euro flights on Ryanair. I booked us a cheap Airbnb in the nineteenth arrondissement. He said he would be my tour guide, as he had lived in Paris in his university days, which were short-lived, he said, university wasn't for him. We explored his old neighbourhood in the poor end of the eighteenth, then went to Montmartre, then to the heart of the city, the Eiffel Tower, the Arc de Triomphe, the Louvre. They don't have Diana of Ephesus at the

Louvre, just the huntress. I made a point of finding her nonetheless but did not see my boyfriend's mother in that rendition.

Our flat had a double bed and it was a treat to have air between us while we slept. When we made love on that trip he started calling me a slut. I noticed, of course, but felt neither aroused nor offended. I merely observed as the fantasy unfolded behind his eyelids, as the word, repeated as if to himself, propelled his pebble of a heart to beat faster, the blood flushing to his cheeks, everything swelling with the excitement of a depravity that was not really there. I squished my tits together, arched my spine, and threw my head back to see if I could believe in it, too.

Once we had seen it all in Paris, we returned to the south and settled into a more usual life in his home. He had some bureaucratic work to do to enroll for his unemployment benefits, and once that was set up he took to his regular routine of reading and gaming in the morning and going for a long walk in the afternoon before dinner, cooked by his mother. They were a harmonious pair. They barely spoke but moved around each other in the way of long-married couples, with acceptance and care. She would smile at me politely and avert her eyes. She spoke English poorly, and my French was no better. After my initial surprise that a man in his forties would live with his mother, once I was immersed in it, their living situation seemed completely natural—in fact, it seemed ideal. She received some money from her deceased husband's pension, which he supplemented with his income from the cruise ships and his unemployment insurance. He paid a modest monthly sum into a household savings account and kept the rest for himself. She did the laundry, the cleaning, the cooking, and the dishes, and in return he provided companionship and occasional IT support—he would download music for her, upload it to her iPod, help her with various difficulties on her email and Facebook. I slid uneasily into this dynamic as her household assistant, though I took my orders willingly enough.

The electricity in their house wasn't grounded. I discovered this one day when my boyfriend's mother asked me to set up her computer speakers—he was on his walk and she didn't know how to plug them in to the back of the computer tower. The lights were off in the computer room, there was just the glow of the screen. She was sitting in the leather computer chair with an earbud in one ear. She rolled it back and pointed under the desk. I got on my knees, fed the cord down behind the desk, and angled the tower so I could see in behind. Despite her incessant cleaning, there were dust bunnies everywhere. I held the tip of the auxiliary cord like a cigarette between my index and middle fingers and squeezed my hand behind the tower, my cheek pressed again the desk's particleboard side. When I found the input with the tip of my finger, the metal plate on the back of the tower sent a zap through my arm. I tried to pull away and sit up, smacking my head on the underside of the desk. With each miss of the cord, hunched over in that space, I got a sting, until it finally clicked into place and I pulled my hand back. When I crawled out backward and turned around, his mother was just sitting there in the computer chair, humming away to the Bee Gees. When I moved aside, she rolled the chair in to the desk, her right hand already extended, reaching for the mouse.

In the third month of our time there, my boyfriend's brother came to visit. He was older, balding, and he spoke only in French, though he was perfectly bilingual. I gathered this fact when I overheard him on the phone to a prospective English employer, barely a trace of an accent, though I never heard him speak English again. He was between jobs, spent many hours in his room on his laptop, and did very little around the house. For some time, I had been responsible for the ironing. Their mother said it bothered her hands, which were becoming arthritic. She held up her bulging knuckles so I could understand. By that point, I did not have significant funds to contribute to the household and felt some sense of obligation to offer my labour, though the gendered division of tasks in their home bothered my feminist sensibilities, which I worked hard to repress during that time. When the brother came, his laundry came with him, and entered into the rotation for ironing as well. Their mother brought the basket of clean clothes to the living room, where I set up the ironing board. I ironed, then folded and stacked the clothing according to the owner. When I was done, their mother requested that I also iron the brother's underwear, which I had not thought necessary but did anyway.

I should say that I have a port-wine stain birthmark above my left eye. It is not relevant to anything except what happened next. It was my practice to bring the laundry upstairs to the bedrooms. The brother went out during the day to the café where he liked to bring his laptop to check job ads and send emails, so I typically placed his laundry on his bed. I would bring their mother's laundry to her room, and our laundry to our room, where I would put it away. This day, I brought the laundry up as usual. Their mother's bedroom door was open, so I deposited her things on her chest of drawers, part of an oak five-piece set that was crammed into her room. I brought our clothes into our room and put them away slowly and carefully. If there is one nice thing that stands out in my memory about that time it is the feeling that there was no rush, there was no deadline, no need for efficiency or to get to the real thing I was supposed to be doing. Because I was not doing anything except being, and being, at that moment, meant smoothing the T-shirts with the palm of my hand as I laid them in our drawers, one by one.

The brother's door was closed, which was not unusual, so I knocked, though I knew he was not home. There was no response, so I pushed the door open. The Wi-Fi in the house was poor, but on the second floor, if you stood near a window, you could connect to the neighbour's high-speed internet, which was much faster, for streaming in particular. As the door swung into his room, I saw that the brother had not gone to the café after all. He was sitting on a high stool at his window with his laptop perched on the windowsill, his headphones on. I entered and noticed, too late, as his screen came into view, that he was jerking off. I caught the curve of a thigh, a flick of long hair, a flash of dark wet flesh. A woman lying down, a man standing over her. As I backed toward the door, hoping I could leave before he realized I was there, I stumbled and the laundry basket fell with a clatter to the ground. He whipped around at the noise and only then did I see the birthmark on the woman's face, just the same as mine, on the left side, beside her eye and toward her temple. I looked at him in shock as he tried all at once to close the laptop and pull his pants up. I turned toward the door but looked back as he let out a yelp. In his rush to close the computer, he pushed too hard and sent it over the sill. I heard it smash on the brick in the courtyard below. As I closed the door to his room, he was standing at the window craning out over the ledge, his pants around his ankles.

I left the house quickly for a walk and to run errands for their mother. I didn't see the brother for the rest of the day. When I returned in the afternoon, he was out and he only came home just before supper. It was as though nothing had happened. His laptop was miraculously fixed and he made no indication that he was embarrassed. He met my eye unflinchingly, though he made no more effort than usual to speak to me. I followed his lead and wondered if I had imagined the port-wine stain. In fact, I wondered if I had imagined the entire event.

Most meals in their mother's repertoire involved a deep-fried element. Battered fish was a weekly menu item and it was delicious, served with aioli, slices of lemon, and a salad on the side. That night, as always, we ate together and were more or less merry, though I struggled to push the scene from earlier out of my mind and keep up with the conversation, which was entirely in French. I drifted into my own thoughts as the supper went on. I ate my meal with my usual zest, as I love food and don't ever deprive myself. I believe this irritated their mother, who was very mindful of her weight and would often eat only fruit for supper as we gorged ourselves on her cooking. After, we sat in the living room and drank espresso while the brother looked for a movie on TV that we might watch and their mother did the dishes. When she was done, she placed a sheet over her budgie's cage and whispered her good night with an exhalation of cigarette smoke before curling up in her recliner and popping the lever to kick up the footrest.

As I watched the brother flipping through the channels, an unbearable queasiness hit me in the gut. It felt like a noxious balloon inflating in my stomach that desperately needed to be popped. I fled upstairs to vomit in the toilet. I was formidably sick. After the movie, the family retired to their rooms and I tried to heave silently, to turn the doorknob to the bedroom without a sound and ease the door shut, to make the least amount of noise possible, though I vomited every twenty minutes for the entire night. In the morning I stayed in bed, stomach shrunken and finally calm. I drank cautious sips of water and slept while the family convened for their usual breakfast of coffee cake and juice.

When I emerged in the afternoon I was ravenous and dizzy. I showered and brushed my teeth, then descended to the kitchen in search of food that would stay down. As I stood at the fridge, their mother came into the kitchen and stood behind me, at the sink. When I turned toward her with the orange juice in one hand, the butter in the other, the notion of buttered toast making my mouth water, she came up close to me and took out an earbud, removed the cigarette from her mouth.

"I didn't sleep for even one hour last night," she said. "You inconsiderate girl." Her voice was low and slow. She had rehearsed, it seemed, had deigned to speak English on this occasion. My head flushed hot and dizzy as she left the kitchen in a haze of smoke.

On the Friday of what would be my last weekend in France, my boyfriend and I took a trip to his grandmother's home outside Montpellier. She was ancient, blind, and she had lost her memory and much of her ability to communicate. She sat in her rocking chair on the porch most of the day. Her youngest son was her caretaker and would inherit her house in return, when she died. My boyfriend felt no obligation to socialize with his grandmother, so we dropped our bags and left to meet his cousins and friends from the past.

We walked to the river through tall grass and then forest. Someone had brought a six-pack of watery beer, and I had picked up a bottle of white wine on the way. There were introductions in French and I nodded along, not absorbing names or understanding niceties. There was a tall white woman with an amber tan in jean cut-offs. She had long thin legs and dirty blonde hair cropped to her chin. A Black guy with acne sprinkled along his jawline in a shirt that said YOLO across the chest, his eyelashes so long they appeared to be weighing down his lids. A snivelly white guy with a nasal voice like he needed his adenoids removed, calves like bowling balls. The woman with the tan asked me where I was from, her lips pursed so tightly that the skin around them was white from where the blood was being forced out. I offered her a swig of my wine and she declined. The guy in the YOLO shirt passed her a beer, which she took, avoiding my eyes as she extended her arm in front of me.

At the river I took my shoes and shorts off and waded in with my bottle of wine in hand. It was already down past the halfway point and I wasn't slowing down. My boyfriend asked what I was doing and I rolled my eyes, then peeled my shirt off awkwardly, switching the wine bottle from hand to hand. I hadn't worn a bathing suit and I was in a pair of lacy black underwear and a sheer black bralette. I threw my shirt to the shore and it hit my boyfriend in the face. Everyone was silent, watching us, but I pretended not to notice and turned away, lowered myself in. The cold of the river was sobering. I held the wine high and dunked my head. I felt unhinged, or perhaps just unleashed, pleased with my boldness. As I walked out, I yelled, "Santé!" before slugging back the last sips from the bottle. My boyfriend came over to me and held my wrist. I tried to break free, but he held tighter, his hairy hand a cuff. The woman with the pursed lips looked away. The snively guy crushed his beer can and threw it into the woods. The YOLO guy picked up his backpack and slung it over his shoulder.

That night we went to bed late. As I drifted to sleep my boyfriend felt around in the dark for my body. It was as though I were watching from afar. I watched as he held my head down and thrust into my mouth, I watched as he used the weight of his body to turn me over and get himself off inside me, I watched as his lips sounded out words I couldn't quite hear, and did not want to. I watched as I lay there after he was done. Only when he was asleep did I move back into myself. I showered. I went outside and sat in his grandmother's rocking chair. As the sun came up I went to our room and packed my bag. He was still snoring away in bed. I took a train to the airport in Montpellier and flew standby. I did not say goodbye.

You know when you get a new credit card and you check the expiry date and think, wow, that is so far in the future. And then suddenly you're getting notifications that your credit card is about to expire and you have to update your payment info everywhere. That is the feeling I have had since returning home. That is the feeling I have on this birthday. The feeling that life is accelerating. That, as my body moves through time, each passing moment amounts to a smaller and smaller fraction of the whole, which is my life. That a second now is a smaller portion of my whole life than it was a second ago. Everything seems shorter, faster, more urgent. When I leave my new house for the spa, this sense of acceleration overwhelms me. I lock my door and step over the stain of cat blood.

It is a silent spa. You can talk in the front office but nowhere else. There is a door at the end of the entry hall with an illustration of a mouth with a forefinger poised in front of it, shushing you. In the waiting room there is no talking. There are signs on every door and every wall. You can't talk in the float tank, not even to yourself. It is not allowed. They tell you this when you come in. You can't even talk in the stairwell leading to the room the tank is in. If you forgot to ask a logistical question, too bad. The woman at the front desk has burgundy hair chopped into a sharp angle pointing to her chin and shaved up the back. She tells me that I will shower before entering the tank, I will use the earplugs provided to protect my ear canals from the salt, I will use the Vaseline provided on any scratches or cuts on my body. I must not forget this step, as the stinging will be unbearable and will only get worse as time goes on. There are over 1,000 pounds of salt dissolved in the water in the tank, so I must not urinate or bleed, as it is a labour-intensive and costly process to drain, clean, and refill. I will be charged up to $2,000 if I excrete any bodily fluids in the tank. Then she laughs.

"But I'm sure you won't do that," she says.

People find it meditative once they adjust, she tells me. The room will be dark except for the light from the tank, which will go out when I close the lid. I can leave the tank open at first, if I need to. Some people need to. It is normal to become disoriented. I can use the foam pillow if my neck gets sore—some people find they can't relax their head. They can't trust that their head will float like the rest of their body. They can't trust the tank. Most importantly, enjoy. She leads me through the waiting room to the stairwell. She opens the door to the stairs, she points at the sign with the finger on the lips that says, "Shh!" and she turns, mimicking the gesture as she makes meaningful eye contact.

The light in the tank is the LED blue of the outdoor Christmas lights suspended in the dark of leafless trees downtown at night. The lights are off in the float room and the tank is open, aglow, the water lapping at its mouth. She shuts the door behind her. I take my clothes off and climb in. I forget to shower, I forget the earplugs, I forget the Vaseline. I slide in and lie in the water. I pull the lid closed above me and at first it is perfect. At first I am weightless, cradled in absolute darkness, moored by the salt, the walls, the lid, the silence. I breathe deeply, like I am meditating, and I think, this is it, this is the moment when everything will become clear, when everything will change. This is the moment of revelation. This is my moment. The moment stretches into minutes, into half an hour, and then my neck aches, a cut from shaving my bikini line burns, the water presses the silence into my ears, and I feel nothing, nothing at all.

Blue like the Sky

You are at the dinner party with your new girlfriend. I arrive late to the long table. There are ten people seated, eleven including me, and the table is full of food displayed on ornate china dishes, a chaotic bouquet of peonies, and two silver candelabras, one at each end. There is an empty chair for me and I sit, one seat down from you. You are across from your new girlfriend, who is blocked from my view by the bouquet. I try to get a glimpse of her face, but I am already seated and it would be weird to stand up again just to see what she looks like. I can see the tip of her bun over the flowers, her graceful wrist as she reaches for a dinner roll, and I know I am lumbering by comparison. I clear my throat, sure that my voice will come out shrill and rasping if I speak. My hands are moving clumsily like I'm wearing baseball mitts, like that feeling first thing in the morning when it's hard to make a fist, extremities still thick with sleep. Maybe you liked tiny, elegant people all along.

I decided to wear all blue to the party. Cerulean. Or is it azure? I'm not sure what the difference is. A bright kind of blue. The type of colour that clearly shows stains and sweat. Cerulean corduroys and a cerulean angora cardigan with a darker blue tank top underneath, matching cerulean socks and navy blue boots. As I sit there, conversations swirling in every direction, I wonder at my decision to dress this way. I do not recall my reasoning, or even making the decision at all. But here I am, like a Smurf, or Violet Beauregarde. I notice that your hair is an unusual shade of yellow and feel a bit better. You used to keep it short when you were with me. But you have grown it long and died it like banana candy, the marshmallow type. I wonder if you're hiding grey. You catch my eye mid-bite and we say hello across the lap of the interloper sitting between us. I would like to say more, but the seating arrangement is too awkward and the host is standing to propose a toast, her glass held aloft, the other hand gesticulating. I glance across from you again and your girlfriend's face is newly blocked by the raised glass of her neighbour.

I wrote you an email not long before the party, but before I knew you had met someone else. I told you too much about my life, detailed a recent failed date and my new apartment. Told you I would be back in town briefly, now, to visit my parents. You never did respond. I recall my email as I sit at the table and I wish I had not come. I wonder if I can leave without anyone taking notice. I look at my legs and observe how they are rooted to the chair. Tree trunks and growing. My stomach is swelling under my sweater and my breasts feel suddenly full, pushing over the top of my bra. My throat is being compressed by my chin, an anvil at the bottom of my face, my teeth crunching together. I try to take a breath, and then try to stand, but I am fixed in place, lashed in by the table, unable to escape even if the opportunity should arise.

When we finish eating, your girlfriend stands to follow the party to the living room. Somehow her face is still blocked. First by someone's elbow, then a hanging lamp. But I glimpse her body as she moves toward the door and see that, in fact, it is her abdomen, not mine, that is swollen. From behind me I hear your voice ring out cheerfully. "It was like ordering a pizza," you say. "Bam." The interloper laughs loudly. Your new girlfriend places a hand on her firm, round stomach, rubbing tender circles.

Cap-Rouge

We meet just west of Quebec City. I'm sitting on a bench over-looking the Saint Lawrence. The river is peaked with whitecaps and dotted with hundreds of windsurfers. Bright sails in primary colours attached to little neoprened bodies muscling against the wind. I'm eating spaghetti out of a repurposed yogourt container and his bike shoes make a clicking noise as he approaches. He is wearing span-dex shorts and his calves ripple. He is more than twice my age, hair greying to white. I can tell he's serious about biking by the carbon fibre road bike, the ergonomic helmet, and those gloves that go just partway up on the fingers, with padding on the palms and holes on the back so your hands can breathe.

I haven't spoken to anyone in days and I've been on the road for over a month. Left a boy in a cabin in the woods north of Toronto who I may have loved. Maybe not. He met me there, a last goodbye among the mosquitoes and horseflies. We swam across the lake. We spent hours of every one of those last few days together in bed, then said goodbye on the side of the road. I have an empty feeling that is either heartbreak or relief. Maybe both. Or perhaps it's simply the feeling of driving for hours alone. I haven't been alone for years. Maybe this is all I am feeling. The intensity of silence. I've been stopping at gas stations just to have a conversation. But conversations have switched to French and I'm rusty, can't quite get the words to flow into sentences, certainly can't crack a joke. Nonetheless, I've been buying overpriced bottles of juice and chatting with cashiers.

When he sits on the bench beside me, I clear my throat in case we're going to talk. He speaks in English and I'm pleased. He asks which direction I'm coming from.

"West," I say. My vocal cords feel out of tune and my voice sounds like it belongs to someone else.

"I hope you're going to stop in Quebec City," he says.

We arrange to meet at a bar on a steep cobblestone hill. He has showered, changed into jeans and a white T-shirt. He's wearing Birkenstock sandals and his feet are tanned a rich brown, the arches peppered with wiry black hairs. We sit on the terrace. The bar is full of people who seem cool and happy. Like their lives have brought them squarely to this moment without any effort at all and here they are, in the warmth as the sun sets, reflecting off the windows and off their sunglasses as they drink something nice, skin glowing from the summer sun, freckles on their shoulders, the salt of a french fry on their lips. He orders beer for both of us. He tells me that he rides out past Cap-Rouge every day. That, since he retired, he cycles for his mental health and to stay fit.

The waitress brings our beers on a round tray. Her hair is black and blown out, pulled back on one side. It wisps forward elegantly as she passes us the beers one at a time. She asks if we'd like to order food and I echo the question across the table to him. He looks up at the waitress. "Thank you, but we would like to have a drink first," he says.

He asks me about myself as though he is making a point of doing so. I tell him I'm driving across the country. "I live in Vancouver, but I'm moving to Halifax for graduate school," I say. "Everything I own is in my car or in the back of a Canada Post truck somewhere along the Trans-Canada Highway." I tell him that I've left my boyfriend and my old life behind and I wonder if it was the right thing to do. "A fresh start," I say.

We're both silent for a moment while we sip our drinks. The sun has just dipped below the horizon and the sky is fluorescent pink. I watch his face as he takes another sip. His head is turned slightly, like he is thinking hard about what I've said as he observes the table next to us. His cheeks are covered in silver stubble. His eyes are narrow and long below pronounced eyebrows and his hair is straight and coiffed. An expensive cut. He looks like he should live in the Mediterranean. He has a broad mouth and skin like a Shar-Pei's. The wrinkles in his forehead ripple deep and fleshy. I wonder what it would be like to stick my finger in one, how far in it would go.

"I remarried five years ago," he says. "Sometimes it's best to start again."

He tells me about his new wife. Younger than he is, still working, while he is a retired translator. "For the feds," he says, and the abbreviation sounds stilted in his Québécois accent. She's away for the week, at a conference in Montreal. Their apartment is just around the corner from here.

"Was it over before you left, or were you leaving to end it?" he asks.

"I'm not sure," I say, which is only partly true.

He tells me he has a daughter who must be older than I am. "Children change everything," he says. "You disappear in the relationship, under a pile of laundry, and you're slowly worn down by hormones and the fights and the terror of adolescence." He finishes his beer. "I chose to start fresh, too."

"I was not honest before," I say. "The truth is the relationship was perfect, or it seemed perfect. From the outside, he was nice and considerate, always on time, always willing to give me a back massage." I tell him about how my boyfriend was stingy, and how I couldn't square it because his family was rich. He didn't tell anyone—none of our friends knew—but he had all this money, for rent, tuition, a car, fancy trips. I couldn't wrap my head around it.

"He said it wasn't his money, it was his family's money. And so he never paid when we went out for dinner," I say. He nods his head as I speak, and I wonder if this is a date. "That was always split down the middle. Same with movies and groceries. He didn't even buy me gifts, not even for my birthday." This is the first time I've said any of this out loud, or even made my thoughts coherent, but I say it to this stranger and it feels good. I can't stop. I tell him that all the niceness, and all the money, even though it never quite trickled down to me, meant I had to pretend to be middle class, and clean, physically clean.

"I had to shower every day and clean my apartment before he came over, and I still felt like he was slumming," I say. "Like he was using me to slum." He sips his beer, shifts in his seat, but never breaks our eye contact. "I didn't know how to talk to him," I say. "Being rich is something that ekes into your bones."

I tell him that maybe I left to see if he would follow, or maybe I left because it was the easiest way to end something that could have gone on forever.

The sun is down now, and the waitress turns the heat lamps on. They glow orange above us and the warmth waves down my arms. He orders us another beer and asks if I would like to have dinner at his apartment. He has two rib-eye steaks in the fridge, some garden vegetables, and a bottle of red wine. I feel so flushed from the heat lamps and the beer that I say yes.

We walk up the street and all the buildings are grey stone. The sky is a rich, pillowy blue. He holds the gate open to his apartment building and sweeps me through with a hand on my lower back, up a flight of cast-iron steps, and then through an ornate wooden door. It's a loft, white and minimalist with mid-century modern furniture, all teak and clean lines. A sheepskin rug in front of a gas fireplace. He left a large casement window open and there is no screen. He rushes toward it and we notice mosquitoes on the wall. The window is old and framed in wood. He swings it shut with a slam, fastens it with a curved brass latch in a brass hook.

"I'll get some wine," he says.

I watch him move gracefully to the kitchen, open a cupboard, reach for a pair of long-stemmed glasses. He uncorks the wine with one of those openers that work in a single smooth motion. Not even a flex of the bicep. Not even a pop. As he's pouring, I look at the art on the mantel. A tall, blown-glass vase with blue and purple swirls. One long branch of pussy willows arching out of its rippled lip. A carved antler. Next to the mantel, a large lithograph of a sailboat. I notice a mosquito on the frame, another on the wall next to it, and then another. I look down the hall and see that it is flecked with mosquitoes. Hundreds of mosquitoes lining the wall, top to bottom. I call him to come and see.

"Disgusting," he says.

"We should get rid of them," I say.

He disappears into a room at the end of the hallway. Returns with two books and hands one to me. He looks uncertainly at the insects, then at me, and I take the lead. I hit the wall and pull the book away. Three black smears. He joins me. We are shoulder to shoulder, then bending, swatting diagonally, and then on tiptoes. He grunts. I can smell his deodorant as he lifts an arm to smack a cluster high on the wall. We smack and smack and smack. I can feel sweat beading on my upper lip. My lower back is damp. The mosquitoes squish and splatter. Some get away, but most just sit there as we slaughter them. When we're done, we stand back. The wall is streaked with blood and severed limbs and tiny wings.

"We should wash it," I say.

"Let's go to the kitchen," he says. "I'll fry the steaks."

Today Is
the Day

Teeny is almost five months pregnant. Lucas is the baby daddy and he is bad news. He gave Teeny her first hit of Dilaudid when she was sixteen. He showed her how to sniff, then how to smoke, and then he showed her how to shoot pills. How to crush them up and cook them down. How to find a vein and how to keep everything clean. He showed her how to make money, brought her around to meet his friends. She did the work, he kept the cash. She tried to dump him after she found out she was pregnant. He dropped her off at the abortion clinic and told her to stay out of his life. Teeny waited until he drove away, then walked to Noser's house.

She and Lucas were on and off after that. She went on methadone and he tried to stop using for a while, got on methadone too, but he started buying extra bottles off friends, then had a few dirty urines in a row. This afternoon, Teeny catches the bus across from the Ultramar, gets off at the university, and walks to her twenty-week ultrasound at the Janeway alone. She lies on the table in her hospital smock. She can feel the cold off the pleather examination table through the thin paper beneath her back. The lights are off in the ultrasound room and Teeny stares at the perforated ceiling tiles in the glow of the monitor with a hand on her stomach. The baby is moving, slow pressure across the bottom of her stomach and then a quick squirm by her hip. The tech comes in and gives her a bedsheet to spread over her legs. She rolls the sheet into the waistband of Teeny's underwear as she lifts the smock up over the mound of taut belly. She squeezes gel on the probe and spreads it over her skin. She's silent for a while, studying the screen, angling the probe this way and that. Teeny's heart races. Then the tech turns the screen to face her and shows her the little heart, the feet and hands, fingers and toes. She asks if Teeny wants to know the sex and Teeny nods. The tech points to the screen and says it's a boy. Teeny walks home from the hospital clutching the pictures the tech printed off for her. She stops every few steps to admire his sweet upturned nose. His fist. His perfect round head.

When she walks in the front door of Lucas's apartment she knows he is on the go. The air is frenetic. She walks into the living room as he shoots coke into Jolene's arm. Jolene lives next door and is always up for a party. There are needles everywhere and Lucas is buzzing. He can't sit still. Teeny stuffs the ultrasound photos in her purse and turns to leave, but he flies at her.

A few days later, her mom, Diane, picks her up from Noser's house and drives her to her doctor's appointment. They talk about her methadone and she still has a black eye from Lucas. Her doctor says he will have to contact Child Welfare. He says he would have had to before the black eye anyway, because of the methadone, but hopefully they'll be able to work together to make sure she maintains custody. He says that Teeny has family support from her parents and that looks good for her file. He says she should stay away from Lucas and hands her a list of support services for women in abusive relationships. It's a handwritten list that has been photocopied so many times it's barely legible. He says that if she stays off pills and sticks with her methadone, she has a really good chance at keeping the baby. That maybe the grandparents can share custody and she can have access that way. He is a good doctor, her mom says, after the appointment.

"Knows about mental health, you know?" she says.

The social worker stands on Noser's doorstep two weeks later, her clipboard cocked against her hip. Black polyester dress pants hugging her thick legs. Her hair dyed that reddish purple colour. Noser answers the door as Teeny smears cover-up over the yellowing bruise that runs from the bridge of her nose to her temple. Blends it in with a wedge-shaped sponge stained different tones of beige, disintegrating at the thin end. She hasn't seen Lucas since. Downstairs, Noser shakes the social worker's hand.

"I'm Darlene Doyle," the social worker says, "from Child, Youth, and Family Services."

"Come in, my dear," he says. "Teeny's just upstairs. She's gettin' right big, b'y." He brings Darlene into the living room. Teeny has cleaned. Borrowed a vacuum from her mom and everything. She even lit up one of the Scentsy candles Diane gave her for Christmas. The place smells like cinnamon and cloves over cigarettes and weed. They haven't opened a window in months.

"You wants a cup of tea?" Noser pokes his head out from the kitchen.

"Is Teeny coming down?" Darlene asks.

"Just a sec now." He walks to the foot of the stairs. "Teeny!" he yells. "Missus is waitin'." Then turns back to Darlene. "Sure ye don't wants a cup of tea while ye waits?"

When Darlene Doyle leaves, she drives to Lucas's house to do a risk assessment. It goes badly and Lucas hammers on Noser's front door late that night. Teeny wakes to the sound of yelling. She sits up in bed and shifts her legs over the edge. She sits there and listens to the front door slamming, a car peeling out from in front of the house, and then another car a few seconds later. Noser doesn't have a car, but he's gone by the time she puts socks on and pads softly downstairs. She pulls the curtain back a crack and peers out the front window. The street is empty and quiet. Noser calls her from the lock-up the next day, tells her he won't be home for a while.

Joey comes to stay a few weeks after Noser is transferred to the penitentiary. Noser can't make bail and will have to stay in holding right up until his trial. He and Joey have been friends since they were kids, grew up next door to each other, went to school together, were in and out of jail together after they dropped out. Joey never got into drugs, though, nothing hard at least. But he stole like a magpie. They had a couple weeks of overlap in the pen this time around and Noser told Joey to go stay in his apartment while he was away. Told him to take care of Teeny for him but to keep his hands off her, as though she were part of the furniture, a porcelain ornament, an expensive sound system. Noser calls Teeny to let her know and she answers when Joey knocks. She thinks about how she is like a revolving door to her own life. How all these men are an infinite string of tornadoes tearing through her. Sending her spinning. Wouldn't it be nice if she could shut that door? Wouldn't it be nice if she could put a stopper on the storm? She pushes the thought aside and gestures for Joey to come in. Her stomach is a taut ball perched on top of her matchstick legs.

Teeny goes into labour two weeks later and five weeks early. It's a Sunday in July and Diane suggests they go on a day trip around the bay with Joey. They go swimming at Northern Bay Sands and roast hot dogs on the beach. Joey lights a joint by the fire, and when Teeny tells him to put it out, her mom laughs and asks for a draw. Teeny wades into the ocean slowly and the cold makes her stomach clench up firm. She stays in until she is numb all over and floats on her back, face to the sky. All the sounds of the world muffled by the water.

Teeny starts cramping on the way back into town, as they turn onto the Trans-Canada Highway. They stop at the gas station in Donovans so she can pee and when she stands up to get out of the car, blood splashes from her body onto the concrete like someone has tipped a cup upside down.

Joey sees it happen and wrestles the nozzle back in the gas pump. "Get back in the fucking car!" Joey yells to Diane. "Some fucking load of blood. Get in the car."

He picks Teeny right up off her feet and puts her in the passenger seat, a smear of blood on his forearm. He shoves Diane in the back, gets behind the wheel, and drives like the cops are after him. Teeny yells the whole way. She yells for the baby, she yells to Jesus, Mary, Joseph, and God Almighty to keep the baby alive. She yells for custody, she yells because it hurts like hell, like hell is opening up right there in her stomach, like her whole being is ripping out of her body as blood seeps onto the upholstery and her belly tightens again and again.

In the delivery room, it is too late for an epidural and a nurse offers morphine.

"Get that shit away from me," Teeny says.

When the nurse tells Teeny that it's time to start pushing, she doesn't want to. She says no. She says she wants to stop, she wants to go home. She says she can just breathe through the next contraction, but when the next one comes, it is harder and faster than anything she has ever felt.

"Push through your bum," the nurse says.

"How in the fuck do I do that?" Teeny yells. But then it happens.

There is a nurse on either side of her, holding her knees up to her shoulders, and she is propped right up. She pushes like she is trying to dislodge her insides. The doctor is there then, holding a cloth against her crotch, slowing things down.

"Do you want a mirror?" the doctor asks.

"Fuck no!" she yells.

"I can see the head," the doctor says.

Teeny reaches down to feel what is going on. It is hard and wet. It is prying her open and impossibly big.

"You can't push it back in, honey," the nurse says.

"I'm just feeling," Teeny says. Her fingers feel the baby's hair, they feel that it is real, they feel that she is really doing it.

"Get it out of me!" she cries, as the next contraction comes rushing over her body, and she heaves, tears running down her face, and she feels her soul rending from her body and it burns like a knife between her legs, but she pushes and the head is out.

"Pause here," says the doctor. "Take a deep breath," she says, and Teeny sucks the air in. She looks down and there is his shiny head of black hair. Just there. So close.

When she pushes again, the baby slithers out of her and the nurse holds him to her, legs and arms dangling. He is crying and his eyes are closed, his skin covered in vernix and blood. The nurse plops him on Teeny's chest like it is no big deal, like babies are born just like this one, every day.

The night Noser gets out of the pen he is rotted. He's staying at the halfway house on Garrison Hill. He's rotted about the halfway house. He's rotted about Teeny. He's rotted that Joey didn't do what he said, didn't keep his hands off her. He's rotted that he went to jail for looking after Teeny and this is how she repays him. Teeny's baby is almost a toddler and Joey has been there with them this whole time. Noser is so rotted that he gets up out of bed, walks down past city hall, past the Delta Hotel, then up the hill to Teeny's new spot, and starts banging on her door at three in the morning, then again at six, then again at eight. Then basically all day.

"Come outta there, Joey!" Noser hollers, as he hammers his fist against the door, then the window. "Come out so I can smash your face in!" he yells.

Noser has his shirt off and by noon he is getting a sunburn on his shoulders. He has a teardrop tattoo on his left cheekbone and a shitty tiger over his right pectoral muscle. Joey gave him the tiger tattoo during those two weeks together in the pen. He used a safety pin as a needle and soot, from burning a toilet paper roll inside a shampoo bottle, as ink. Noser has just finished two years less a day for assault, theft over $5,000, and uttering threats. He put on twenty pounds inside. Got sober, worked out every day.

He walks up the steps to Teeny's house again that evening and starts kicking the door. "You piece of shit!" he yells. "You don't belong in there, you filthy fuck."

Teeny sticks her head out the window.

"Get out of here, Noser. Get out."

"You too, you slut," he says. "Come out here and I'll show you."

He's at the same level as the open living room window, but it is just out of arm's reach. He walks down the steps below the window and can reach the sill that way. He tries hauling himself up, the ridges of the window frame digging into the tips of his fingers, but even with all the push-ups he did in the pen, he can't get a good enough hold to get his body up and in. He hollers a string of curse words and Joey comes to the window. When he sees Noser clinging to the sill he pulls out his knife. Noser sees a glint of silver as Joey slashes toward him.

"You think you're gonna stab me!" Noser yells. "Filthy little prick arse." He picks up a cinder block from beside the house and throws it at Joey's face. It smashes through the top part of the window as Joey ducks back in, and glass shatters down onto Noser's head.

A neighbour calls the cops. Two patrol cars roll up and Noser takes off through the yard next to Teeny's house, then through a cut that runs up to Patrick Street. He is gone before the officers have heaved themselves onto the sidewalk. When the big officer with the shaved head knocks, Teeny appears at the window. She doesn't meet his eyes, lights up a smoke, takes a long, slow draw. He asks if there's been any trouble, says someone called in a fight.

"It's all good, just some lunatic shootin' his mouth off," Teeny says.

"How did the window get smashed?"

"He threw a friggin' brick at it," she says.

"Did you know this guy?"

"Never seen 'im in me life."

After a few more questions, the officer lopes back to his car. He stands there, writing in his notepad, speaks into the radio on his shoulder. The sun is setting, reflecting off his sunglasses, and he is a bulky silhouette. The other patrol car drives away. Teeny pulls her head back inside. She reaches up and closes the smashed-out window for no real reason except that it feels more final than leaving it open.

Dive Master

This is everything I know about you: That summer we met you were briefly in love with someone else. I watched you love her and I imagined it was me. You also loved kittens. You played with the kitten I brought back to the dive centre like it was your own precious child. Your lips parted as you held your hand out, your tongue slipped between your teeth as the kitten swatted at you. You had lived in Egypt once before, in this same town, and had come back because the diving was unrivalled, and the people were wry but welcoming, though most divers didn't mix with the locals.

You were nimble underwater. Your long hair fanned out behind you, gold at the tips from the sun. You had wide hips and a flat stomach. You wore an athletic bikini: sports bra and tight shorts. As you pulled your wetsuit over your thighs, there was a moment where your ass would resist the neoprene, and then it would pop into place before you hauled the suit up over your shoulders, untucking your hair, zipping it up over your breasts. On this one dive, we had to swim out to the access point, marked by a buoy, and then drop down. You crossed your arms over your chest. You let the air out of your buoyancy control device so your weights were enough to pull you under. And you sunk. You turned around to check on the rest of us as we panicked down behind you. Your movements smooth and relaxed. Forefinger and thumb coming together in a circle in that universal call and response. Okay? Okay.

When Amelia left to travel down the Nile on a felucca, you came to my room to watch movies and we sat with the kitten playing on my bed for hours. He was a ginger cat I had found meowing alone on the beach, staggering toward the water, just old enough to have his eyes open. You were lying down, so nonchalant, propped up on your elbow, your head resting on your fist. Occasionally, our hands would touch by accident, and each time was a jolt that made me so wet I could barely look you in the eye.

You loved showing me YouTube videos. Your favourites were of people who were colour-blind putting on those glasses that let them see colour for the first time in their lives. Some sixty-year-old dad whose adult kids pitch in and buy the glasses for his birthday and he opens the box with an expression of astonishment. He's holding in his tears and it's that much more moving because it's clear he's not the type of dad who usually cries. Then they all go stand outside. Their mom is filming the whole thing, and she pipes in every now and then to tell people where to stand, or maybe she just lets an "Oh my God" slip out once or twice. When he puts the glasses on, it's this moment of awe. He's obviously crying behind the lenses, and he is just staring at one spot, maybe a tree, or a balloon. Then he points and says the colour. "Green." His voice is shaking and quiet, even though you can tell he's usually a loud guy. "Red." Then he's looking around everywhere and pointing, listing colours. You said there was something so moving and anachronistic about it. This old guy discovering the world with the innocence of a child and crying at the beauty. You would have tears in your eyes, and then you would laugh at yourself and at me. Though I only cried because you did, because your sadness was affecting. I didn't give a shit about the videos.

Underwater off that coast was a rainbow. You knew every fish and sea slug by name. You knew every type of coral. You would bring your camera underwater and document everything. A giant moray eel hissing at you, a Spanish dancer undulating like a red ribbon, thousands of silverside fish swirling in a tornado, an ancient sea turtle putt-putting across the blue. And the entire reef like a giant city: apartment blocks of pillar coral, arenas of brain coral, fields of table coral. You would scroll through all the photos after a dive and tell me about everything we had just seen together. We had sex in the ocean at night. On the shore and then in deep. All the fish invisible out there below the surface. You dug your fingers into me like you were hunting for clams in the sand and the phosphorescence exploded around our bodies. I imagined watching us from above, a radioactive silhouette.

You told me once that you wanted to fuck everyone. Your teachers, your students, your best friend's dad, your best friend's mom, Ethan Hawke, Beyoncé—all of Destiny's Child, in fact—Uma Thurman, me. You could just look at someone and suddenly imagine a world in which you were having sex. You imagined the circumstances in which it would happen. End-of-the-world scenarios. Sex due to disaster. Sex due to tragedy. Stuck in an elevator. Last people on Earth. Drunk at a party. The possibilities were endless. Sometime shortly after that conversation I walked in on you masturbating to naked pictures of Amelia. Instead of feeling embarrassed or turning your laptop off or stopping, you held out a hand to me, told me to come lie down with you. You left the computer open, her face staring at me from the screen as we both came.

We lived in huts in a hostel that was expensive if you were from Dahab but dirt cheap if you were from Canada or the US or Europe or Australia. When Amelia heard through mutual friends that we were together, she got someone to bring all her belongings to her in Cairo and pay her outstanding bills at the hostel. She never did come back. I guess you two communicated then, somehow, though I didn't think to ask. I clicked through her pictures on Facebook in the internet café and wondered if I was prettier than she was. You never talked to me about her, even when I asked, and then I heard that she had gone home to Ontario and I stopped thinking about her, assumed you did too, though her pictures stayed in a folder on your desktop. I had won.

I think you imagined your life like a Wes Anderson movie, or a vintage Fisher-Price dollhouse, cross-sectioned and neatly organized into a pleasing symmetry, all beauty, governed by some divine force. Like you were an actor, or a doll, and not, in fact, responsible for anything you did. Not in fact responsible if a giant child's hand picked you up and used your unwitting body to knock down everyone in your path.

You fucked me in the bathroom of the hostel bar. I was pressed up against the sink and you buried your whole face and your fingers in me until I cried out. Later that night, sipping a beer outside at a low table, lying back on the cushions, you told me you wanted to go to the butterfly forest in Mexico. You told me the butterflies clustered on the branches by the millions. That when they slept they were like mussels on a pier, dangling from the trees. But up close, they were these quivering clumps in the dawn, ephemeral, squishable. You told me we could go together. After seeing the forest, we could spend months diving off the coast.

We moved into a double room at the hostel. We split the drawers: you got the top two, I got the bottom two. Put both our toothbrushes in a cup on the window ledge. I hung a mosquito net around the bed and we lay under the canopy, gazing out at the sky through the open window. You took me for supper at the fanciest restaurant in town. I watched your face when you played with the ginger kitten. I imagined it was our baby and this was how you would look, admiring the creature I had made.

That same week we moved in together, you went out alone one night and didn't come back. Our modest whitewashed huts surrounded the dive centre. It was this open space, with terracotta tiles, a front desk to register or rent gear, a compressor and a repair room to refill tanks and fix stuff, a freshwater tub to rinse the salt off, and a place to store wetsuits, fins, shoes, masks, BCDs. A couple couches and tables for doing coursework or just hanging out. In the morning, I woke early to find you at the dive centre, prepping a class for a dive. You were standing by the gear rentals, zipping up someone's wetsuit, and when she turned around I saw how beautiful she was. Deep black hair tumbling down her back, skinny neck, thick eyelashes. I didn't ask where you had been because I already knew.

I got drunk after dinner and brought an Israeli academic back to our room. I leaned up next to him at the bar, where he was sitting with a local, talking about the bombing on the bridge the summer before. When he turned toward me, I asked if he wanted to leave with me. I didn't bother with small talk. I thought how perfect it would be for you to barge in on us. But you didn't come back that night either, and there I was, with this worm of a man running his hands over my body, telling me I was a goddess, pressing into me over and over. I asked him to leave sometime in the early morning. He told me he couldn't believe what an amazing night we'd had. I wandered through the streets searching for you, returned to our bed. The cat came in through the window and curled up on top of me.

You came back the next day like nothing had happened. She had left and you were with me again, all caresses and sweet kisses. I kissed you back, tried to convince myself that your returning was still a victory. We went for a dive in the moray garden. Waded out along the sandy bottom. You held my hand as we went under. Eel after eel popped out at us, opening their mouths in silent objection at our intrusion. Then you beckoned me over to a big crack in the reef. I went up close and peered in. A giant moray eel raged out at us, then careened backward, huge but afraid. She yawned her jaws wide, fangs bared, her head twice the size of mine, her wrinkled body this massive brown muscle, flexing to six feet long, maybe seven. I cowered and held tight to your arm. Your laugh bubbled out around your regulator. You took it out as the eel retreated, took mine out, and kissed me, exhaling into my mouth so I could breathe.

When we got back to our room you asked me for a haircut. You wanted me to shave your undercut and trim your dead ends, fried from sun and salt. You borrowed an electric razor and proper haircutting scissors from a friend. We put a chair outside on our four-by-four wooden deck, and I wrapped a towel around your torso, tucked it in at the shoulder. I ran my hands along your forehead, your temples, the nape of your neck, slicking all your hair up into a ponytail with an elastic. You sighed and closed your eyes. I can feel your skull under my palm like it was yesterday. I buzzed your undercut short and neat. Then I took the scissors and placed them at the base of the ponytail, on the other side of the elastic, the head side. With one quick stroke I sliced it off. It lay flaccid in my hand as you reached back, a hoarse cry coming from your mouth as your hair fell in an uneven bob around your cheeks. I held the ponytail out in front of me as you stormed through our room, throwing all your stuff in your duffle bag, slamming the cupboard, slamming the door.

I looked you up on Facebook for the first time recently. I clicked on the picture of your wife, and then through her pictures of the two of you snorkelling, the two of you with a puppy, the two of you on your honeymoon in Egypt, the two of you and your newborn baby. You're gazing at it with your lips parted, tongue slipping between your teeth. You are the same—your hair is long again. But your skin is older, wrinkled at the eyes. I still have your ponytail in a box, along with my snorkel and mask, some other odds and ends from Egypt. A statuette of the Sphinx, a bottle of sand from Mount Sinai. I held your ponytail up to the window. It shimmered in the sun, such a beautiful shade of gold at the ends. I held it up to my nose and breathed in. It still smelled of you, and of the ocean, of salt and wind.

La Foule

Jasmine lives with a painter. He sequesters himself in his room, and when he comes out, a haze of paint fumes trails behind him. His breath reeks of booze and cigarettes. His name is Lionel and his room is a wreckage of brightly painted canvases, empty wine bottles, and cigarette butts. His paintings are stacked against the walls, piled high on the dresser, waiting under the bed. In the late 1990s his work was exhibited at the National Gallery in Ottawa, and then in the early 2000s at the Venice Biennale. It was even said that his art captured the zeitgeist of the new millennium. Now he paints wild fauvist portraits and still lifes in frenetic shades.

"French violet and indigo," he says in his thick Québécois accent. "Chartreuse and mauve." Rolling the *r*'s in chartreuse lethargically.

Lionel is in his late sixties, skin dark and wrinkled, fine lines puckering around his eyes, pleating his brow. Dirty stonewash jeans hang from a leather belt off his bony hips. French doors divide his room in two—a solarium where he paints off the front and his bedroom at the back, the door directly across the hall from Jasmine's. His is always closed. He has lived in the apartment for decades, and the living room is a midden of paint palettes, dried tubes of oil paint, empty containers of oil medium, sketch pads, art books cracking at the spine. Jasmine keeps all her belongings in her bedroom. She doesn't dare put her books on the bookshelves in the hall or hang her pictures on the walls because Lionel is very particular. She doesn't even clean, lest it throw off his workday, ruin his groove. If a reference book or paintbrush is moved, he is derailed for weeks.

"Osti de câlisse," he says. "I lost my muse."

Then the drinking begins in earnest. He hides wine in paper coffee cups, puts vodka in his Thermos. Jasmine doesn't notice he's drunk until she gets close enough to smell it oozing from his pores.

Before she moved in with Lionel, Jasmine lived with two roommates, Shelley and Michel. In the months leading up to her departure, three unpleasant incidents took place: First, Michel brought home an armchair he had found on the curb and lugged up Park Avenue one painful step at a time. As it turned out, the chair had been discarded because of bedbugs, whose subsequent infiltration of their apartment was comprehensive. Jasmine coated the floor of her room with diatomaceous earth, filled plastic Rubbermaid containers with the stuff and placed the legs of her bed in them. She spent her spare time blasting the cracks in her floorboards with a steamer. The bites were unbearable. Rows of swollen, bleeding pockmarks up her back and down her legs.

Second, in the loneliness and isolation brought on by the infestation, Jasmine started sleeping with Shelley, which she found to be awkward and unsatisfying, as Shelley was not, in fact, particularly interested in sex with women. On the last night they spent together, Jasmine stole into her room after Michel had gone to bed. Shelley was working at her desk and Jasmine crawled under it. As she slid a hand between her thighs, slipped her tongue where it was warm, Shelley let out a moan, and then pushed her away.

"I don't like head," she said, which was news to Jasmine.

Shelley opened her top drawer and pulled out her strap on. She handed it to Jasmine and they moved to the bed. There were no hands or mouths, not even eye contact, just plastic against skin. Jasmine crept out once Shelley was asleep.

Third, late that same night, in a frenzy of post-coital insomnia and anxiety, Jasmine ate an entire brick of Michel's cheese. It was an aged cheddar, the type that's so good it has crystals in it. She ate the whole thing standing in the cold light of the open fridge. Michel was angry about the cheese, and Shelley was angry about Jasmine in general, or maybe just about the sex. Instead of dealing with any of it, Jasmine moved out.

Jasmine's room in the new apartment is painted coral pink, and there is no chance she will sleep with Lionel, who doesn't cook, leaving no quality cheeses to tempt her. Her bedroom is next to the front door and her window faces onto the deck. Rusting cast iron and a steep set of stairs lead down to the tree-lined street. The smell of linden trees wafts in through her window. She subsists off fifty-cent samosas and cheap thali plates.

Lionel has a daughter, Sabine. She is stunning, with Lionel's complexion and bright green eyes. She is collected, always dressed business casual in a two-piece suit or a tweed skirt with brown nylons, a big purse, and subtle lipstick. Powder pink or lacy peach. One night Lionel comes home so plastered that he can't get into the apartment. Jasmine wakes to the faint sound of scraping metal. In the morning Sabine knocks loud and early. Lionel is still asleep, and when Jasmine opens the front door, she notices scratch marks next to the deadbolt, where Lionel's key had repeatedly missed its mark. Like in a nightmare when you can't quite get where you're going. Sabine breezes past her with an air of derision. She doesn't knock on her dad's bedroom door before letting herself in.

"You live in a slum," Jasmine overhears her saying to Lionel. "Grow up!"

The following day, Sabine brings groceries and puts them in the fridge without saying hello to her dad. Jasmine eats the food, as Lionel is only interested in liquids.

Sabine was born in Alma, in the Saguenay valley. Alma was a mill town, and until the Quiet Revolution, francophones couldn't get decent work, especially if their skin was as dark as Lionel's. He was often unemployed, but when Sabine was born on a sunny afternoon in 1972, he got a job at the CEGEP teaching art. He had his first show at a gallery in Quebec City when she was three. Muted realist paintings. A throwback to early modernism.

When Lionel met Sabine's mother, Marie-Claire, she was wearing bell-bottoms and a sheer mustard-coloured tank top. She was sketching with charcoal down by the river on a folding easel propped on a picnic table. Her drawings were terrible. But her copper hair glistened in the sun, she had freckles on her shoulders and on her eyelids, and when Lionel looked at her lips he was weak with desire. She didn't shave her armpits, which he thought was sexy and slightly embarrassing. After she gave birth to Sabine she wanted to go back to work right away. She was an orderly in the geriatric ward of the hospital, but Lionel said no, even though he didn't have a job and they were broke until he got the gig at the CEGEP.

Marie-Claire was not made to be a housewife. She didn't clean. She liked to smoke pot and sketch. She would boil the blossoms from the honeysuckle in the garden just to smell their sweetness in the house. She spent an entire welfare cheque on a fur coat from the thrift store instead of buying groceries. Marie-Claire loved French music and would belt out the words to Édith Piaf or Charles Aznavour songs while she watered the basil. Lionel would rant about the mess around the house. They would fight and he would slam the door to his studio and paint. But when they remembered they were in love it was like the first day they met. They would laugh and kiss as Sabine danced in the glow of their happiness.

Marie-Claire died in a car crash when Sabine was in kindergarten. Teal Camaro crumpled into a twist of metal around the telephone pole in front of the house. That was when Lionel developed a taste for vodka. He could add it to anything and drink at any time of day. When he drank, colours took on new life. A nose could be turquoise. A cheek could be burnt orange. After Marie-Claire died, Lionel painted the colours from those times before. His reds were the flush of her lips. His oranges, golds, and browns were the glint of the sun on her skin. His pinks were her navel, his greens were her eyes. But a broken heart is always broken, and one day, while Lionel watched Sabine stamping in a puddle, picking up an earthworm, he decided they would move to Montreal.

Jasmine wakes to the high-pitched beep of her alarm clock. She turns it off and wishes there were another body in bed to curl around. She would give anything not to go to work. It is spring, and when she squints her eyes open, the sun is bright through the window even though it's early.

She drags herself to sitting, and then to her feet, pulling on a T-shirt, hoodie, and shorts. She opens her bedroom door and finds herself looking into Lionel's room, his door ajar across the narrow hall. She is surprised to see the door open. She is surprised to see a fire at the foot of his bed. Jasmine pulls the door to her room shut behind her and closes her eyes tightly. When she looks again, Lionel has appeared from the kitchen with an unlit cigarette dangling from his lips, a coffee carafe full of water in hand. Without a word, he walks into his room and pours the water over the flames. Nothing happens.

Jasmine says, "Your bed is on fire."

"Bien, je sais," says Lionel. He has wine stains in the corners of his lips.

"It's on fire," Jasmine repeats.

Jasmine has always planned for a fire. As a child, she would coordinate escape routes while she fell asleep. She would plan how to rescue the hamster and the dog, which precious belongings she would grab on exiting, which window would be best to crawl out of. She knows about not opening the door if the doorknob is hot. She knows about stop, drop, and roll. And she knows that when her grandma lit her mantelpiece on fire, she panicked and fanned the flames. Jasmine knows not to fan the flames.

"Your bed is on fire," she says again, her voice shaking.

Jasmine runs to the living room, grabs blankets, and throws them on the bed. "I think we can smother it," she says. She searches the kitchen for a fire extinguisher, Lionel trailing after her, but she can't find it. She pulls coats off the hook by the door and lays them on the flames.

"I think it's smothered," says Lionel.

They are standing shoulder to shoulder, looking down at the bed. The pile of blankets and clothes is smouldering. Grey trails of smoke leak through buttonholes and lapels, out of pockets and up through hoods. Then, as if fortified by their audience, the flames jump through the fabric, spring from the crack between the mattress and the wall. Jasmine bends to see under the frame. Lionel's canvases are alight. A fauvist inferno beneath the bed.

"Shit," she says.

When Jasmine stands up her head is engulfed in smoke. She hunches forward and dials 9-1-1 as Lionel heaps more clothes on the fire, still trying to smother it but feeding it instead. Blue and red flames eat through the mattress. Oil paint fumes waft through the room. Jasmine covers her mouth with her arm, her eyes watering. Lionel stares into the heat, his face pale. The bed is a pyre and the flames lash the ceiling.

"The paintings," says Lionel.

"They'll be fine."

"There's so much smoke."

"The fire truck's coming."

"The paintings," he says again.

"We need to get out," says Jasmine.

Lionel lunges forward, reaches for a canvas on top of the dresser. A woman's face in cyan, fuchsia, and cobalt. The walls are catching and the ceiling is on fire. Jasmine grabs Lionel from behind, wrestles him out of the room.

She drags him onto the front deck. They are coughing. Jasmine is dizzy. Their feet are bare on the rough cast iron, and as they watch Lionel's window they hear it cracking against the heat. Lionel scrabbles down the stairs. Smoke licks up the side of the building. Jasmine races to the apartment above to warn the neighbours. She hammers on their door and they answer in their pyjamas. They rush down the steps, one carrying a computer tower, the other a banker's box.

"Five years of research," she hears him saying.

Jasmine gazes through her bedroom window at the laptop she bought with all her savings. She takes her sweater off, wraps it around her fist, smashes the single-pane window with a punch, widens the hole with a second punch, and then crawls in. She slices her thigh on a shard of glass sticking out of the windowpane and wipes the cut with her sweater. Droplets of blood follow her into the room. The door leading to the hall is closed and she launches her things out onto the front deck. Computer, keys, wallet. Smoke is seeping in around the door frame and she can hear the sirens.

"The paintings," Lionel calls up from the sidewalk.

Jasmine climbs out again through the window, wary of the edges this time.

"Forget the paintings!" she yells.

There is a sharp pop and Lionel's window shatters. Glinting shards of glass rain on the concrete below as the apartment takes a deep breath. A pause. Then an incendiary exhale. Flames leap up the stucco, igniting everything they touch. Neighbours spill into the street. The fire trucks pull in. Jasmine barrels down the steps clutching her belongings, the cast-iron treads digging into the flesh on the bottoms of her feet.

She turns in time to watch as the apartment lets out a high-pitched wail and all the colours of Lionel's paintings fight in the flames, a frenzy of clashing tones pouring out the window, melting in the heat.

Corpus Christi

There are only two weeks until the end of exams, but Blake Peach can't focus on studying, it's that hot out. He staggers out of the library after his spare block. Christina is waiting for him by the front steps of the school. Their backpacks are heavy and they squint into the sun. Blake is wearing his thick uniform pants and black Doc Martens. His legs are itchy with the heat. Christina holds on to his shoulder as she peels off her black tights, her legs now bare under her kilt. Blake strips down to his black singlet. His arms are pasty and thin. The heart Christina stick-and-poked on his chest is partly visible above the low neck of his shirt. The tattoo is still red and tender around the edges. He swings his sweater over his shoulder as Christina shoves her tights into her backpack, jams her bare feet back into her shoes. They cut up behind the penitentiary toward the pond. At the top of the hill they can see right over the city. Little houses and little cars and little lives. They can see the Catholic grave-yard back the way they came and the Protestant graveyard across from it. The tombstones like spent matchsticks stuck haphazardly into the ground.

The pond is a backup reservoir and No Swimming signs dot the perimeter. They find a sheltered spot, far from the trail. Groggy from studying, they don't have anything to say to each other. They don't have their bathing suits with them, so they swim in their underwear. Blake jumps in and Christina wades slowly. The rocks are jagged and slimy underfoot. The water washes away the day, the cold brings their bodies back to life. Blake treads, waiting for Christina. She swims over, wraps her legs around his hips, and he holds on, runs a hand up her waist. He wants to keep her there longer, feel every part of her. He slips a hand down her underwear and cups her crotch. She pulls his hand out, pushes away, and swims out far. Blake watches her, then gets out, sits on a rock, and lights a joint. The water makes Christina's body the colour of rust and distorts her movements, makes her limbs all wavy as her head bobs up and down and her legs frog and kick, frog and kick. She swims back, pulls herself out into the heaviness of the air. She stands over Blake and shades her eyes. He passes the joint up and she takes it with wet fingers.

"I feel so fucked up about the whole Father Murphy thing," she says, inhaling deeply and holding her breath for a second at the top. She passes the joint back down.

"I know," Blake says. "It's all so weird." He takes a puff. He can feel his first toke tingling in his fingertips, weighing him down even more than the heat.

"Like, how could he do that?"

"It's fucked." Blake coughs and holds the joint up, but Christina is looking out over the water.

"It's also just fucked how many people knew."

"He's such a scumbag. I'm glad he left before I had him," Blake says. "Do you want more?"

"No, thanks." Christina waves the joint away. "Not one of them did anything."

"I always thought he was gross." Blake spits on his finger and thumb and stubs the cherry out in the pool of saliva, pulls out the charred nub and flicks it into the pond, twists the roach off and puts it in his backpack.

"You know Roy Anderson is my cousin," Christina says. She's looking down at him again, her hand flat over her eyes, shading her face from the sun.

They fall asleep on the rocks and Blake's arm goes numb under Christina's neck. The sun beats down on them. Her head moves to his chest. His heartbeat drums through her.

A decade earlier, Roy Anderson came home for his older brother's wedding. The night before, NTV had broken the story about Father Murphy, and in the intervening twenty-four hours, it had been picked up by every news station across the island. Someone had gone to the media with an anonymous complaint. They had dates, names, and specifics, and although the media didn't release them to the public, everyone knew in that silent way so common to the island, kept all the hearsay stored in the backs of their minds. Roy caught a cab from the airport and stopped off at Lottie's to surprise Clyde at his bachelor party. The party was already well under way when Roy's plane landed, and everyone was talking about Father Murphy. They were saying people had complained for years, they were saying everyone in town had known, a formal report had even been made. They were saying the report had been buried. The Church and the cops made sure it never saw the light of day. No one said Roy's name, but everyone was thinking it.

Roy Anderson had moved to Ontario right out of high school and enlisted in the military. He left the island in his dust. As a teen he had been lanky and hunched, with greasy long hair that hung in front of his face. He and Clyde had been the only kids at Corpus Christi from Virginia Park. A friend of their mom got them in. Everyone else lived in the catchment area and had big houses with fenced-in yards, two parents, and two cars. In the end, the one thing Roy's mom ever did to give him a better life was the thing that messed him up most of all.

People at Corpus Christi said terrible things about their mother, versions of the truth, which was that she was on welfare and lived with her two boys in housing. She would bring men home and rub whiskey on the kids' gums to keep them asleep while she made extra money to pay for groceries and pot. Between getting stoned, drinking with the bikers, making money and sometimes dinner, she didn't have time for the kids. So Roy spent a lot of time alone, roaming the streets listening to Fleetwood Mac over and over on the Walkman he got for his birthday. That Walkman was Roy's prized possession. His mom said she got it at the pawnshop, but there was no way she could have afforded it. Roy didn't ask questions. He just popped the tape in and pulled the headphones over his ears.

When he heard about the wedding, Roy Anderson was stationed in Afghanistan. He wasn't invited because he hadn't come home since he was seventeen, and Clyde didn't think he would want to now. Plus, Roy was messy. But he wanted to surprise his brother. He thought maybe it was time to make amends, reconnect. When he walked into Lottie's, no one knew who he was. Lisa Squires looked him square in the eye and went back to talking to Ricki Roche. Not even a glimmer of recognition. It was loud and "Sonny's Dream" was playing. Everything was the same. Roy pushed through the crowd to the bar. He took a shot of Jameson and washed it down with a swig of Black Horse before scanning for his brother. Clyde had come to visit him a few times in Petawawa, and again when Roy transferred to Gagetown. They had partied on the base, but they never talked about the past. Roy spotted Clyde, bought him a beer, and shouldered his way over. He came up from behind, gave his brother a hard punch in the arm, and held the beer out.

"Holy fuck, it's Roy," Clyde said.

"You thought you'd get away with not inviting me, you little shit," Roy said.

"Never misses a beat," said Clyde.

They hugged and Clyde seemed like he might cry, then slugged down the beer Roy had handed him.

"Listen, we got to talk," Clyde said. But it was so loud and people were pushing against them. Charlie Aylsworth was yelling Roy's name over and over and pointing at him, and Roy was shaking hands, popular, or maybe just novel. Certainly handsome in a way he had never been before. The city, the whole island, was hungry for new people, even hungrier for a homecoming. So Clyde let it go and the gossip about Father Murphy got quiet for the night, moved out of earshot, with that skilful secrecy of a place that has had to protect itself against all odds.

That week, Roy relaxed into boozy nights and lazy days. He couldn't drink in Afghanistan, where he had been on duty every waking hour. He had wanted to drink himself into oblivion ever since he changed out of his uniform and got on the plane back to the island. That part of this place had never left his blood, and smelling the salt air made him want a drink even more. He finished an eight-pack of Blue Star every night and smoked a pack of cigarettes every day. He liked finishing the beers and the cigarettes and starting fresh in the morning. It gave him a sense of purpose. He'd walk to the corner store, hand over the cash, put the beers in the fridge for four o'clock, peel the plastic off the pack of Player's, snap up the foil, and smoke his first cigarette as the coffee brewed. Clyde was an electrician and left for work at eight a.m. Becky, his fiancée, was a nurse and when she wasn't working a shift, she was sleeping, so Roy barely saw her. He was on his own in the house all day, and after coffee he would roll a joint, smoke it outside with his shirt off, nap in the sun, nap in front of the TV, maybe look at porn on his phone. He had packed a couple books with him, but they sat unopened on the coffee table. A Mark Twain novel and a murder mystery. Too ambitious for a holiday.

On occasion, once the sun went down, and after his first few beers, Roy would head to Minty's. He'd buy coke off the bikers at the bar, sometimes pills. It was during that week that Roy Anderson got all the news about Father Murphy. First from the TV at Minty's, and then from Micky O'Reilly, who sold him blow. Micky moved in different circles from Clyde's crowd from Corpus Christi. He was low down on the ladder with the Vikings and Roy had seen him smash a young guy's face in against the Dumpster behind the bar.

Micky glanced up at the TV. "Sick fuck," he said. "He'll get a knife in the side if he ever sets foot in the pen." He sipped his beer, one finger wrapped around the mouth of the bottle. Micky O'Reilly didn't know who Roy was, didn't know Roy was watching the TV feeling like his guts were hanging out, on display for the whole island, the whole damn country to dissect. Roy didn't flinch, didn't turn his head. Not even a twitch in response.

Micky hated pedophiles as much as the next person. Or maybe he just hated gays. "My sister was attacked on the mainland," he said. "I went and found the guy, kicked 'is face in. Not a tooth left in 'is mouth when I was done."

Roy Anderson drank his weight in beer that night, spent every bit of cash he had on coke, and didn't stop when the sun came up. He staggered into the gas station on his way home for his case of Blue Star, pack of smokes. When he got to the front door of Clyde and Becky's house, Becky was just getting home from her night shift, key in the lock. She jumped when she saw him, just over her shoulder.

"Jesus, Roy," she said, clasping her heart.

"Becky, b'y," he said.

"You scared me."

"Where the fuck is Clyde?" he said. "Where the fuck was Clyde when I was a kid?"

"You need to go to bed, Roy."

"Not looking out for me," Roy said. "That's where he was." He stumbled through the doorway and fell face-first on the couch.

Blake Peach stays away from the old Corpus Christi Catholic school. It's up behind the lake and the road is overgrown now, brambles and knotweed shielding the school from view. The building is starting to fall apart. A piece of the roof has caved in on an old classroom, most of the windows are smashed out, the walls all have water damage, and the ceilings are brown with mildew and mould. In the auditorium, there's a mattress on the floor. It's stained and soggy. There's a firepit next to the mattress and garbage everywhere. Broken bottles, chip bags, and cigarette butts. The emergency exit door is broken off at the hinges and the piece of plywood that once covered the opening has been pried away. The school was condemned in '98, after repairs from a flood revealed asbestos in the walls and lead in the water. That was the same year it was going to go non-denominational like all the other schools. "A toxic environment," the PTA argued, and then they started lobbying for a private school, tuition based, to keep the Catholic education in and the riff-raff out.

In brighter days, Blake's father, Jim Peach, went to school there. His father's father went there, too, and his father's father's father before that. When Corpus Christi closed down, the priests transferred to the new private Catholic school, Lakeview, where Blake goes now. Some of those priests have known the Peach family for generations. Father Francis says the Peaches are an upstanding family—hard-working, athletic. Blake likes Father Francis. He's ancient and wrinkled but always shakes Blake's hand when he runs into him on the street, like Blake is a real human, not just a kid. Blake steers clear of some of the other priests. Father Kavanagh has notorious halitosis, and Father Vincent has scaly patches of eczema on his hands and around his nose that flake off in sheets. Father Murphy was transferred to a parish around the bay when Blake was in grade one, but everyone had known to stay away from Father Murphy. He looked too long, got too close.

Lakeview is on the other side of town. Out of sight of the old school. It's next to the cathedral and, contrary to its name, has a view of the ocean. The exterior is brick and glass. It has a rotunda and fancy landscaping out front with ferns, wooden benches, and cedar mulch. It is shiny and earthquake resistant, with whiteboards instead of chalkboards. Free from the past. Almost.

Blake has been accepted to Saint Mary's for the fall on a partial basketball scholarship. Christina got into McGill, and they're going to try long distance. That summer they spend most of every day together. Then it's August and the days are getting shorter again. There are whales at the mouth of the harbour and the blueberries are out. When they kiss, Blake savours every texture and every taste. Goes back in his mind to that first time. It was like this: Blake backed up against the side of the shed and tried to focus on a feature of Christina's face, but it was too close to see. It was New Year's Eve and the party in the shed was loud. She unzipped his parka and reached under his shirt to find skin, her hands cold against his stomach. Blake was nervous, like he didn't want her to think that he thought this was serious, or like he felt as though someone might come around the corner and find them. And even though he was drunk, he could tell he was acting weird, holding himself stiff. He could tell by the way Christina looked at him. When they kissed, he felt frantic, as though he were trying to find some truth between her molars, solace in the back of her throat. Blake had never been in the ocean—too wild, too cold—but she tasted how he thought the ocean would taste. He could feel the bass vibrating through the wall of the shed at his back and he pulled her in.

Now Blake wonders how it will end, what their last kiss will be like, if he'll feel sad. He is pouring himself a bowl of cereal after supper and his father, Jim, is watching the news when the anchor announces that there is going to be an inquiry into Corpus Christi. They call the whole scandal Corpus Christi. Like it wasn't a school. Like it was only ever a scandal. They're saying that it wasn't just Roy, and it wasn't just Father Murphy. The news anchor says seven boys have come forward, men now. He says two priests have been suspended and are under investigation. He says only now, ten years after the news broke, have they got witnesses willing to testify.

Blake's phone dings. It's a text from Christina.

are you watching the news?

ya

the other priest is Father Francis

ffs how do you know?

mom's friend works at the CBC

Blake puts his phone down and stands in front of the TV with his bowl of cereal poised at his chest. The news anchor has moved on to the weather, a hurricane in the forecast. Blake picks his phone back up.

I don't believe it. He hesitates, then presses Send.

Blake's dad flicks the TV off.

"Jesus Christ," he says. "Let sleeping dogs lie." He rubs his hand over his face.

Blake drinks the sugary milk in the bottom of the bowl and wonders if Roy Anderson knows. Later, he hears his parents talking in the kitchen.

"Father Francis is nearly ninety," his dad says.

"How that boy got himself in that situation is another question," says his mom.

"Let the man die in peace."

"But what if it had been Blake?"

Jim is silent.

"In the end, it's none of our business," his mom says.

By the next day, the news about Corpus Christi is overshadowed by the storm warning. This isn't just any old hurricane. This hurricane is forecasted to be the most destructive storm to strike the island since 1935. They are saying this is the new normal. This is climate change. They're saying hurricane season will get earlier and fiercer and longer. They call it Estelle, category three. When Blake googles "category three hurricane," it says, "devastating." Strong enough to break windows, tear off roofs and doors. Uproot trees completely. Estelle ravages Jamaica and Florida. They are expecting it to nick the island in two days. They are expecting flooding. People screw plywood over their windows. The shelves of the grocery stores are picked clean. Blake goes to the store at the end of the two-day countdown, but there is not a bag of chips to be found. Home Depot runs out of sandbags. The weather woman swoops her arm over the green screen demonstrating the trajectory. Maybe it will miss them. Maybe they will just catch the edge, some rain, a tropical storm. However, she says, this is unlikely, then swoops her arm again, draws circles in the air over the city with all five fingers, swoops her arm off to sea.

Christina was just seven years old when Clyde and Becky got married. She was a flower girl, a crown of daisies in her hair. The background of their invitations was a silhouette photo of them as Bonnie and Clyde, back to back, holding their hands as pistols. Roy nursed his hangover from Minty's for two days, then it was the eve of the wedding, the rehearsal dinner, and then the day of. The ceremony was at the cathedral. Clyde wore a bow tie. Becky wore a simple white dress, trumpet shape, the bridal saleswoman called it—tight down to the thigh, and then fanning out to the ground.

The reception at the country club was fancy, verging on flashy. There was an open bar, generous, or perhaps ostentatious. The caterers served finger food, and the cake was three tiers, with buttercream roses in baby pink and Creamsicle orange swirling down one side. The speeches were short, and by the time the sun went down, the drinks were flowing and the dance floor was full, stilettos kicked off in favour of bare feet. Clyde and Roy's mom spent the night hovering around the bar. She was wearing pleather heals and a purple polyester dress from Suzy Shier with a droop neck. After a passing hug, Roy did his best to avoid her. Retrieved drinks from the opposite side of the bar. Did not make eye contact. Eventually, she was so drunk she just sat on a bar stool, swaying to the music, staring out at the room as she swilled another gin and tonic.

Roy Anderson and Lisa Squires did shots of tequila alternating with salt and lime, then danced fast to "I'm Still Standing." They were laughing and sweating next to Becky and Clyde. Roy thought, *Maybe this is it, maybe I can live here, maybe it's all going to be okay.* Roy and Lisa took a break for more tequila, a quick trip to the bathroom for a bump of coke. When they came back they went straight to the dance floor. They danced through "Billie Jean" and "Footloose." When the music slowed to "Georgia on My Mind," Roy swept his arm up and over his head, extending a hand to Lisa, and then pulled her in. They stayed that way for "Can't Help Falling in Love."

They stumbled off the dance floor together. Outside was a warm night and they stood apart from the crowd. Roy Anderson thought how beautiful it was—all the people in their sequined dresses and their ties against the city lights.

Lisa was drunk and high, and she couldn't coordinate her fingers to flick the lighter. "God, I'm such an idiot," she said.

"You're radiant," Roy said.

"Stop."

"I'm serious."

"You're too much," she said. And then she asked, "How are you so nice when all this shit is going on?"

"What do you mean?"

"Like, just everything with Father Murphy and the news, just all this shit everyone is saying," she said. "You're so brave."

Roy didn't know what to say, so he didn't say anything. He chugged his beer, sucked on the cigarette.

"Like, I can't believe he was a child molester this whole time," she said. "It's just gross."

Roy stepped on the cigarette.

"I have to go to the bathroom," he said. On the way past the crowd at the door he caught the word "pedophile" in the jumble of conversation. He went to the bar and did three shots of tequila in a row, followed by a beer.

Some people were saying Father Murphy had given him the strap too many times and too hard, some people said it was touching in the confessional, and some people said it was the worst stuff you could imagine.

Roy stumbled back on to the dance floor and yelled, "Father Murphy can rot in the hell God made for him!" his beer held high.

Clyde and Becky were dancing, Becky with her shoes off. Everyone stopped moving and stared as Roy ranted about shovelling dead bodies out of an abandoned warehouse in Afghanistan the month before. Said he had fucked every whore he laid eyes on. Said, "Fuck Corpus Christi." Clyde moved over to him, took his arm gently. Roy flicked him off with a force that took Clyde by surprise.

"And you," he yelled at Clyde as his brother reached out again. "What did you do? You looked the other goddamn way. Didn't that work out well?" He pushed Clyde off his arm again. "Country club membership, a nice fucking life."

Clyde looked down as Roy reached out toward him, like he was going to hit him, or maybe hug him, but Roy tripped and Clyde stepped back. Roy's beer bottle flew out of his hand and through the air in an arc, smashed on the dance floor as Paul Simon crooned "Diamonds on the Soles of Her Shoes."

Roy Anderson only visited his mom once on that trip home, the day after the wedding, hungover again and impassive. She still lived in the same suite in Virginia Park, the place done up with lace curtains and draped valances. There were ceramic cats in the window and a wall decal that said, embarrassingly: "Home." Roy thought it looked like a label. Or maybe a memory aid to remind her where she was. Or maybe it was for him, a sign to let him know what this place was supposed to be. She had a spider plant hanging in a macramé holder in the corner and puce rugs lining the halls. When Roy came in she was on the couch in jeans and a chenille sweater, smoking a cigarette and reading *People* magazine.

"What a sin about Michael Jackson," she said.

Roy hadn't spoken to his mom in three years. She made him coffee and they smoked together while she read him the headlines. Then she put the magazine down.

"He was a pedophile, though," Roy said.

"Father Murphy's finally gone," she said. "Can't believe they kept that pervert around so long."

"You should have kept a closer eye," Roy said. Then he finished his coffee and his cigarette and he left. He left Virginia Park, and then he left town altogether. He left without saying goodbye to Clyde, without saying goodbye to anyone. He hitchhiked to the ferry and caught a bus back to Gagetown on the other side.

Over the next few months, the stories about Roy Anderson and Father Murphy got more and more detailed. An affair. A long-standing relationship. But Clyde said to Becky that those stories were bullshit, cruel because they had been poor and Roy had always been called a fag in high school. It's never a relationship when it's with a child, he told her. Father Murphy was transferred to the parish around the bay by the time Clyde and Becky got back from their honeymoon. A resort in Maui, hiking volcanoes, snorkelling with dolphins. And people lost interest. The names Father Murphy and Roy Anderson didn't pass anyone's lips for years.

After Estelle has blown back out to sea, it is bright and calm. The sun rises over the harbour, the ocean is smooth and still. Christina walks to Blake's house. Their neighbourhood is up from the lake and the coast, and houses up here are dry enough, even though roofs and siding have been torn away. Christina passes a storm door on a lawn. Yard furniture is displaced in the road. Trees are upturned, root systems sideways. Outside Blake's house there is a deck in the road, and a two-by-four has come down hard on his parents' car, the windshield smashed, the hood dented. A maple tree has tipped into his neighbour's house and the top floor has caved in. The chimney sits on their front step. Christina knocks on Blake's front door and it strikes her as strangely formal, like doors are no longer to be relied on for keeping things out. Blake slips his shoes on and they head down to the lake to see the wreckage for themselves. On their way down the hill, water rushes out of overflowing sewage drains, pours down river streets. The lake has flooded up over the trail, up over the Dominion parking lot, over the road, all the way up over the Catholic cemetery. Cars are submarine, sump pumps are immersed, sandbags lie under feet of water, basements are swimming pools, and memorabilia float, released from the bonds of storage. A doll here, a book there. Blake and Christina stand on this new shoreline, and then pick their way along, toward the cemetery.

"My mom said Roy has to come back to testify," Christina says.

"What?"

"For the trial," she says. "She told me he has to come back 'cause he's been identified by another witness. Apparently, he has to testify whether he wants to or not."

"For the trial?" Blake asks.

"Yeah, the trial," Christina repeats. "Father Murphy and Father Francis. More people keep coming forward."

"But the storm must have slowed things down," Blake says.

"It was already happening," Christina says. "My mom said Roy's on mental health leave because of it. She said he finally had his life together, and now he has to come back." They're walking up on the slope now, just above the cemetery. The grass squelches and their feet are soaked. Nothing is draining.

"My dad thinks they should just let sleeping dogs lie," Blake says. "He said Father Francis is almost ninety and they should just let him die in peace."

The graveyard is on a steep hill and they can see where the flood-water runs into the slope. They can see a few rows of tombstones above water, then a few with water lapping at the base, and then a few partly submerged. A cross with its arms and head rising from the flood, an angel with wings spread wide, water up to her waist, like a bird coming in for a landing. The rest of the graves are underwater now, and still. Blake thinks about the bodies, drowning after they're already dead.

"That's fucking dumb," says Christina. "What's his problem?"

Blake flinches.

"And what about Roy?" she says. "What about all those kids who didn't get to be kids? And didn't get to be safe 'cause of some sicko?"

She pauses. Out of the corner of his eye he can see her staring at him, waiting.

"And what about the Church?" he says.

"Fuck the Church. It's not fair, Blake. Your dad is wrong. He's wrong."

"I didn't say I agree."

"But you didn't say you don't."

"I don't know," Blake says. "Father Francis was always so nice. It's hard to believe."

"Doesn't it make you wonder about every interaction you've ever had with him? Doesn't it make you wonder how many other kids there have been," she says. "Plus, you don't get to not believe."

They've come to the crest of the hill, behind the penitentiary, and they see cop cars down below.

"Maybe it's just better not to dredge up the past," Blake says.

"Maybe it's good we're going to different schools," she says.

Blake is shocked, wonders where the conversation is even going. Wonders if this is just an excuse for Christina to end things, or if this is serious enough to her on its own. He doesn't really care about Roy. He doesn't really care about any of it.

"Listen," he says. "I don't want this to come between us." As he hears these words coming out they sound dramatic, but he can't tell what she wants, and then the sirens are going on the cop cars and he's distracted by the scene. The road the cars are on is flooded. Water right up to their chassis. An ambulance is coming down the street slowly, water up over the bumper and rippling out behind it.

"What's going on down there?" Christina asks, her anger eclipsed by curiosity, though she thinks for a second how this has already come between them.

An officer is holding a roll of caution tape and a pylon, but when he tries to set the pylon down it floats, and there is nothing to tie the tape to. As Blake and Christina approach, they see a body floating in the water. The paramedics are there now, wading toward it and pushing a stretcher. They hoist the body up easily, and it's not right. It is stiff and desiccated. Not bloated, not heavy or fleshy. On the stretcher, it is dark and skeletal. Blake and Christina are close now, and the paramedics are talking to the police.

"It's not a fresh body," one of the paramedics says. "It looks like it's been here for ages."

"It must be from the cemetery," the other one says. "Must have washed out with the storm."

Another Angel

The girl loves waking early because of the way the sunlight hits everything at an angle that makes it all glow, and because it is still quiet. The children are asleep, and even though the others are up and working, there is a silence before breakfast, as bodies warm up and eyes become wakeful. A softness to footfalls, a mutual avoidance of contact and conversation that is not rude but courteous. The courtyard will be busy in a few hours, but for now she is the only person. A brood of hens scratches and pecks for food, a trip of goats chews idly.

It is just after dawn in early spring, the end of March, and it will be a warm day when the sun is all the way up. There are buds in the trees, nodules of life at the tips of the sycamore and mulberry. Crocuses and daisies are poking out between the cobblestones and tall grass. The girl has brought the buckets of water and her hands are stiff. She is resting for a moment, sitting on the stoop overlooking the courtyard, rubbing the fleshy parts of her palms before she starts the washing. The angel is barely visible in the sunlight. Glimmering gold, more of a feeling than something the girl can see. A warm shiver, shimmering in the shadow of the house across from her. It is almost indecipherable, a blank spot in her vision, but then she catches the glint of a wing, the shine of a cloak.

The commission is to be finished within the month and the master has told the young painter that he is to complete the angel, the trees, the ocean, and the mountains rolling into the horizon. A boy is modelling the angel. He sits for the young painter and he is striking. His hair falls in copper locks over his shoulders. His skin is fair and smooth. His forehead high and proud. The young painter and the boy have been friends for months, as the master works on the painting and the boy hangs around the studio, sometimes modelling, sometimes mixing paints. They all admire his beauty, none more so than the young painter. The young painter likes the boy's big brown eyes, he likes how earnest they are. And he likes him kneeling, holding the branch of fragrant white lilies extended in front of him. The smell is sickeningly sweet, masking sweat and pungent oil medium, but the young painter breathes it in with relish. When he paints the boy holding out the lilies, he imagines he is on the receiving end of his gaze.

The young painter has been studying birds, alive and dead, big and small. The parakeet and the hawk, the thrush and the hooded crow. He has observed the staggered tiers of feathers, the individual barbs, the bend of the wings, the musculature, the aerodynamics, and he has exacted the wings of the angel. The young painter extends these wings from the earnest boy's back. He lays down layer upon layer of paint, feather upon feather, barb upon barb, and the angel is luminescent. His wings are real wings and they shine just how the wings of an angel should shine.

Sheila and Diane have come to Italy on their annual trip with their husbands, Richard and Hank. Sheila and Diane have known each other for over thirty years. They worked together for almost two decades at the corporate offices for Effective Plastics in Loveland, Ontario, and since retiring, they have been dragging their husbands to a new destination every fall, the shoulder season, a bit cheaper, and the weather amenable in most places. Last year they went to Mexico for ten days. The year before it was Scotland, the year before that, Holland. Sheila and Diane insisted on walking through the red-light district at night. Dick and Hank were deeply engrossed in conversation about the stock market as they strolled past the women in the windows. It was the first and only time Dick and Hank exchanged more than cursory words.

Sheila and Diane had decided on Italy while in Sayulita the year before, as Sheila recuperated after a debilitating bout of gastroenteritis. The trip started with the Amalfi Coast to wind down, drink wine, and relax on the beach, after which they took a train to Rome, where they spent a full day hopping on and off a double-decker tour bus, the next at the Colosseum, and the third at the Vatican. They have finally arrived in Florence, where they will spend three days doing galleries, cathedrals, restaurants, and boutiques before they catch their flight home to Loveland. They have carefully planned their itinerary and have booked their hotel close to the Ponte Vecchio, where they walk at sunset on their first evening after checking in. They have all showered and changed and are heading out in search of supper and perhaps, Sheila says while Dick holds the door and they all file out into the cobblestone street, some of that pistachio gelato. "I'm an addict," she says.

They walk over the Ponte Vecchio. All the shops are closing up and ramshackle but beautiful, with wood awnings, corrugated wood garage doors, and black iron hinges. They walk over the next bridge so they can look back at the Ponte Vecchio, its buildings dangling above the river.

Diane gasps. "Oh," she says, "how magnificent."

The sun is low and the windows of all the buildings on the bridge and lining the road glow. The buildings are reflected off the river in their shades of peach, ochre, mustard, and burnt orange. The water is absolutely still and the reflection is an underwater world mirrored perfectly back up at them. You could dive in and swim along those streets. Sheila takes out her iPad and lines it up for a photo. She is standing next to a young couple with their backs to the view, smiling into the screen of a phone. All along the wall of the Ponte Santa Trinita, people are craning for photos of the Ponte Vecchio. Sheila leans back to see the full picture on the screen a bit better and taps hard to take the shot.

The girl lives on the farm with her parents and her mother's side of the family. Their houses encircle the courtyard, and they work the surrounding farmland with several other families, cousins who live beyond the second olive grove. She is to marry in the summer, but she avoids the thought as she labours at the washing, the cooking, the cutting and splitting of wood during her last days here. Her monthly bleeding began for the first time two weeks ago, and she can feel a cramping and a fullness she does not recognize but associates with that first and horrible experience.

The girl did not expect to see an angel this morning, which otherwise has unfolded like every other morning. The angel has been sent by God to deliver a message to the girl. He is one of His archangels, and he is excited to talk to a human, something he has only done on one other occasion and with someone who was not nearly as beautiful. He stays in the corner for a while, invisible, and watches her as she rests, as she rubs her hands, as she observes the chickens clucking, pecking, scratching. He did not expect to find her so lovely. She has clear brown skin and dark hair pulled into a braid that hangs down over her shoulder. Her eyes droop low at the corners like a puppy's and are rimmed with dark lashes. Her cheeks are flushed and the angel can see that she is strong. She looks right at him and he knows that she can see him. As he glides toward her, the girl finds she cannot move. She is mesmerized and frightened but cannot turn away as he glistens through the morning, becoming more solid, more gold, his wings like the giant wings of an eagle folded behind him. She feels her heart flutter, her palms become moist. She feels like she will weep, for he is beautiful and ageless.

Sheila and Diane have big plans to visit the Uffizi Gallery. Sheila has been anticipating the sight of Botticelli's *The Birth of Venus*, da Vinci's *Annunciation*, and Caravaggio's *Medusa*, all of which she found out about when she googled "best works of art at the Uffizi gallery in Italy" late on the first night of the trip. She found it hard to read the iPad with her reading glasses, so she read overtop of the frames in the white light of the screen while Dick snored beside her in their hotel room in Positano. She read about the labial symbolism of Botticelli's clamshell. She read about da Vinci's collaboration with his master, Verrocchio—da Vinci painted the angel, while Verrocchio painted Mary. And she read about how Caravaggio's interest in physiognomy influenced his depiction of Medusa. She fell asleep in the glow of the iPad, neck cricked forward on her pillow, glasses slipping down to rest on her chin. Her dreams were supernatural.

They wake early. Sheila blow-dries her hair with a round brush and a diffuser, notices her grey roots are coming in already. She went a shade lighter for the trip. The stylist called it champagne blonde. Dick pulls on his khakis and his Tilley hat. They want to beat the lines at the gallery.

Sheila and Dick are filling their plates at the breakfast buffet as Diane approaches. She is wearing flip-flops and Hank is not with her.

"Hank's feet are too sore," she says.

Hank is recovering from gout, and the red wine and pasta have triggered a relapse. Diane wants to come to the gallery, but she decides to stay with him instead. They'll go shopping, then find a nice café where they can drink cappuccinos and read, she says. She is working on the first of Elena Ferrante's Neapolitan Novels, which her daughter loves, but she cannot quite get into.

"And Hank—well, Hank has a copy of the *Economist*," she says.

They eat breakfast together and Hank joins them as they are standing to leave. Sheila swings her black patent leather backpack over her shoulders, and Dick fastens on his waist pouch. "The gypsies are known to be pickpockets," he says.

Sheila shushes him. "Dick, that's racist," she says. "They're Roma."

The young painter and the boy sit on a low stone wall outside the studio as the sun sets. The young painter has completed the commission and the boy is done in the studio until another angel is needed. The young painter tells the boy that once the paint has set, the piece will be sent to the framers and eventually it will hang in the new palazzo going in on Viagrande, if ever construction is finished.

"It will be the most beautiful painting in the palazzo," he says. "Because your face is the most beautiful face."

"Only because you painted it," says the boy.

The boy listens attentively as the young painter describes the palazzo in lavish detail, entirely imagined but perfectly plausible. The young painter watches the boy's lips, his hands, the glint of his hair, and as his pulse quickens, the extravagance of his descriptions intensifies.

They stroll along the river, glassy in the blue of early night. The young painter places the flat of his hand, ever so gently, on the boy's shoulder as they walk back toward the young painter's room in a lodging above the master's studio. Inside, the boy sits on a makeshift settee draped in red satin. His knees are together and he leans forward, his hands tucked under his thighs. The young painter pours the boy a glass of wine, as the master once did for him. The boy finishes the glass and the painter pours him another. Waits until the boy is smiling, his eyes squinting, then kisses his lips for the first time. Runs a hand through his curls. The boy's shoulders are stiff and the painter squeezes them until the muscles relax into his embrace.

The angel presents the girl with a branch of the sweetest, whitest lilies she has ever seen. He is so caught up in the dark line of lashes running around her drooping eyes that he forgets to tell her what he was sent, by God, to tell her. Forgets to speak altogether. She is innocent and perfectly curious. She extends a hand for the lilies, but he slips his other hand into her palm instead. She looks at their clasped hands, feels his warmth pulsing up her arm. She leads him into the house, past the mezuzah on the front doorpost, down a dark hallway to a small room. The only light trickles sparely through a window above a narrow bed in the corner on a low wooden frame. Her clothes are scattered on the floor. She kicks a dress and her underwear under the bed and closes the bedroom door because if her mother finds them together, the girl will most likely be killed, stoned, she thinks, but it is worth the risk because this angel, this angel is something else entirely, and she does not want to get married in the summer, and maybe, somehow, this will change her life. She takes her clothes off and stands in front of him. Her skin is dark and smooth as silk. As she strokes his wings, revelling in the power of the muscle under the fronds of airy feathers, he wonders if all humans are as sexy as she is. The blood in her cheeks runs so close to the surface, mortality the sweetest temptation.

She wakes to the sun shining hot through the window. Her mother is calling her name. The angel is gone, but the girl's body is shimmering, and the air around her quivers still in his wake. She closes her eyes and can feel the angel's caress. A trickle of gold leaks down her thigh.

The young painter and the boy spend every day together. The painter is no longer young. The boy, too, grows older, is no longer a boy. He models less and less. But he is an apprentice now. Spends long days in the studio with the masters, begins to paint skylines and foliage in their works. He studies hard, watches closely every brushstroke.

One day, four years after their meeting, the painter begins a new piece, and the new model is very young, so delicate and fine. His lush sandy hair frames his sharp jaw perfectly, and the skin on his arms is buttery and soft. He poses for the painter in the afternoon light, shadows softening around his lean shoulders and neck. As the painter helps the new model into position, like the master once helped him, he moves a hand over the new model's back, and then over his thigh. The new model is to kneel, gaze up reverently at an imagined dove, a baptism. The painter presses against the new model and inhales the smell of his youth. The door creaks open, for the old model, who was once a boy, has brought the paints, freshly mixed. The painter does not notice the old model at the door, watching as he strokes the new model. The old model takes a sharp breath and retreats quietly, takes the palette with him.

That night, the old model writes a letter detailing the offences of the painter, his love of young boys. For sodomy is illegal, he knows, punishable by death. He slips the note into the tamburo in the Palazzo della Signoria and hurries off into the night. He does not look back.

It's 9:30 a.m. and Sheila is sitting in a darkened room with one of Leonardo da Vinci's earliest paintings—*Annunciation*, she reads on the placard, one of the paintings she has most anticipated seeing and read about on the internet. There is a large padded bench from which to observe the painting and the room is very dark, except for the spotlights illuminating the soft skin of Mary and Gabriel. The gallery is packed with people, mostly taking pictures or resting on the crowded bench. She finds a spot, places her backpack beside her for Dick to sit when he arrives. Dick is slow in galleries, and she can never tell if it's because he is so interested, he is taking his time, or if it's because he is so bored, he lets his mind wander in the hope that he will forget where he is. She sits in that hush that falls in museums and cathedrals and libraries.

Sheila is struck by the painting, by the strangeness of the perspective, its odd angles that don't quite make sense, by Mary's unnatural hand gesture. She is struck by the painting because, she thinks, it tells the origin story that is the backbone of the religion that upholds the moral code, for better or worse, of the past 2,000 years of life in the Western world. She can look at it and she can suspend her disbelief in God (which she does not talk about with Diane because Diane is a staunch Protestant), because her back is sore and here she is on a padded bench in Florence—Florence, for heaven's sake—and why not just let God be real? And there is Mary in the courtyard in front of her house, and behind her the trees, the water, and the mountains rolling into the horizon. And she is draped in sumptuous fabric that gathers around the waist and fans out and it's red and blue and she is beautiful and fair-skinned, and when Sheila's daughter was a girl she would have loved the look of her. The angel Gabriel is kneeling before Mary, Mary the mother of God, and he is luminescent. His wings are real wings and they shine just how the wings of an angel should shine and he is holding out a branch of lilies and he is telling her, goddammit, that she, she herself, will bear the son of God, who is actually also God, and who will change the course of history forever and ever and ever. And Mary has these funny hands and a bent-up pinky finger, but she is saintly, she is a goddess, she is divine.

Dick enters the darkened room and scans for Sheila's blonde bob. He walks toward her slowly, and when he sits down between her and two preteens sharing a headset, listening intently to the gallery guide, Sheila leans into him, loops her arm through his. Dick is silent as he takes in the painting. Sheila rests her head on his shoulder.

"It's a good thing Diane took Hank shopping," she says. "I can't see Hank enjoying this."

New Chelsea

"If he wanted to see other people, he should have just said something," I say.

"Do you want a cappuccino or an Americano?" Mina asks from the kitchen.

"He just keeps screwing me over," I say. "Cappuccino, please. When will I learn?"

Mina appears in the kitchen doorway. "When you have sex with someone else," she says. She holds up a baby pink milk glass mug. "Is this mug okay?"

Mina has an espresso machine, because, she says, coffee is a priority. She froths the milk until it's shiny and pours the cappuccinos.

Last week I bumped into her in the grocery store in town. "Come up to New Chelsea with me," she said, when I told her about Derek's most recent infidelity. "You need to get away," she said. "Plus, I need help getting rid of the giant hogweed."

New Chelsea is an old fishing town turned cabin country. Where there used to be farmland and fishing stages are now fallow fields and saltbox houses redone with white vinyl siding gone grey from rain and dirt. A lone cow lies in the grass above the beach. It's like everything here is waiting for something to happen again. For the cod to come back. For everyone to remember how great it is to see the stars and smell the ocean. There are only five kids in New Chelsea. We drink the cappuccinos at Mina's dining room table. In the middle, a yellow Pyrex bowl filled with monochromatically yellow damson plums. A vase of daisies on the window ledge. Mina has the house just so, milk glass everything and vintage plates with a black floral pattern around the edge. Mina's family is from the west coast of the island. Some of them came here from Ireland, some of them were here from the start.

"If you see these plates at the thrift store, get them for me," she says. "I'll pay you back."

She has resuscitated the 1950s rose print linoleum that was under beige carpet and added an unexpectedly perfect piece of contrasting geometric linoleum to bridge the threshold from mud room to dining room. Melamine countertops. Wallpaper in all different patterns and art on every wall. The windows are antique single paned, wavy in places from gravity on silica.

"We're going to need the caffeine," Mina says. "Giant hogweed disposal is a big job." She has brought rubber rainsuits for us to wear and leather work gloves that go to the elbow. She has two welding masks to go over protective goggles, a massive pair of shears, and a plastic barrel for storage.

"He said he had to leave early from the party," I say. "He said he was so tired he had to go to bed." I pull the rain pants on over my jeans. "I should have clued in when he kept checking his phone. Then I saw him on Water Street with his hand cupping Eli's neck. You know, in this really intimate way. It wasn't there for long, but you could tell exactly what it meant," I say. "He's such a homophobe, I was surprised, to be honest. But I didn't say anything, just that I thought he was going home. Do you think I'll be too hot in all this?"

"We're definitely going to be sweating." Mina passes me a raincoat.

"Then Eli posted this picture of them eating Cheetos in his kitchen that night." I pull on the raincoat, then my boots, and then these thin disposable booties overtop. "Then a photo of their brunch together the next day."

"He's a literal piece of garbage," Mina says. "Here, put these under the leather gloves." She hands me a pair of latex gloves. "You can't be too careful. This shit can burn."

"I looked at pictures on the internet," I say.

"Make sure every bit of flesh is covered." Mina buttons her rain jacket to her chin and pulls on latex gloves, safety glasses, welding mask, then leather gloves. "How's this?" She turns around with her arms out. "DIY haz-mat," she says.

The path that runs from the house to the brook is narrow and loamy, winding down to the water with roots underfoot. You can hear the brook from the house, loudest from the master bedroom. We walk in single file, Mina in front. We're each holding one side of the barrel. Mina has the shears. The air smells like pine needles and cut grass. A willow arches overhead.

"You know he asked if we could try role play," I say.

"Oh God," Mina says. "Hang on, I have to adjust my grip."

"It was so lame," I say. "He basically just wanted me to shave my pubes and to slap me like we were in some shitty RedTube video."

Mina rolls her eyes and takes off one set of gloves so she can get a better hold on the barrel. We both switch hands.

"It wasn't even hot," I say. "He was just slapping me and pulling my hair, and then he came." We keep walking. "Honestly, it was painful in the least sexy way. Just enough to be unpleasant and without any of the allure of actually feeling like he had control over the situation. But what do I know about that shit anyway? Totally not my thing."

"It's just here," Mina says. "See that huge one with the white flowers?"

"I'm so sweaty," I say.

The hogweed is over six feet tall. We pull our welding masks down over our faces. Mina uses the shears as I hold the stalks, and then I place them carefully in the barrel, trying to avoid doing any unnecessary movement, trying to avoid shaking the flowers and spreading the seeds, trying to avoid making any contact with my body, even though I am completely covered, not one iota of flesh exposed. When we have razed the plant to the ground, we seal the barrel and carry it to the pickup. We strip down and place our clothes in a fish pan, careful not to touch our bodies. We jump off the truck in our underwear and clomp to the brook in our boots, kick them off on the rocks, and wade in. We float on our backs and stare at the trees and the sky.

"Do you think he feels bad?" Mina asks.

"I hope so," I say.

"You have a red mark on your chest," Mina says, swimming over to me. She stands to inspect the splotch forming below my clavicle.

"Shit," she says. "You're supposed to wash it with soap right away if it's from the hogweed."

On the internet, I learn that the sap from giant hogweed causes photodermatitis. If the sap gets on your skin, you can't protect yourself from the sun in that spot. Like a vampire. If the sap gets on your skin and then you go in the sun, you get burns that bubble and rage. Wikipedia says that the blisters form within forty-eight hours, that black, brown, or purplish scars can last for years. I wash the lesion. It's the size of a penny and hot red. I cover it with gauze and duct tape to keep it in the dark and wait. When I leave New Chelsea, my hair is crusty from swimming in the brook, and the burning blister on my chest has popped, leaving a raw patch right above my heart.

Whippits

In Dallas's bathroom there was pink and black mould around the rim of the bathtub, the type that grows under the caulking. I should say it wasn't just in his bathroom. All our bathrooms suffered this same affliction. In fact, his was better than most. Dallas's family only had one bathroom and there was no shower curtain. This was back when we were all poor. I suppose we still are. His sister was huddled up at the top of the bathtub when I came in, with her knees tucked into her chest to cover herself, her arms wrapped around them. We both averted our eyes. I think I said hello, or maybe I said sorry, as I tried to pee silently and contain the smell of sex that was wafting up from my crotch. When I wiped, the toilet paper was streaked with pale pink. I had just lost my virginity. As though virginity were a mitten on a bus. In reality, it was an albatross, the only remaining obstacle between me and womanhood. I had to convince Dallas to do it, that it was meaningless to me. Which of course it was not.

There were three housing projects in the neighbourhood and we all lived in the worst one. Most of the old rental houses in Strathcona had been torn down in the sixties. But the projects they put up were no better than the ramshackle dumps of yore. At least they used to be stand-alone houses, with tall peaked roofs overlooking gardens and clotheslines. Those rentals they tore down would be heritage houses now, redone with beautiful clapboard and plaques on the side. The new units were a bunch of rotting boxes, all stuck together with cookie cutter yards the size of postage stamps, stinking carpets, not enough space, and zero privacy.

I pulled my pants up without standing all the way. When I clicked the bathroom door shut, Dallas was waiting for me in the hall, and his mom, Barbara, was standing in the doorway to her bedroom with a look on her face like, *What is this white girl doing in my house?* Though maybe that was the voice in my head, not hers. In reality, she probably felt sorry for me, or didn't care. But when you're sixteen, you think all eyes are on you. My own parents were never around. My mom left when I was a kid, and my dad worked at the chicken factory when he was clean, didn't come home when he wasn't. I wasn't used to an adult looking me in the eye, so when Barbara stood there like that, I leaned into Dallas and gazed at the floor. My vagina was sore. Like when you hold your mouth open at the dentist and the corners get all stretched and red.

I spent more and more time at Dallas's that year. My brother went away to juvie, and there was never any food in the fridge at my place. Dallas's fridge was always full, nothing fancy, but there was always food. They all cooked on different nights, and they all ate supper together. At first it made me uncomfortable eating with them, everyone talking, sometimes laughing, other times fighting. When they teased each other it didn't cut to the core, it didn't incite violence, it was mostly just gentle joking, and then everyone would get in on it. That was my first experience of banter. Not like they were a perfect family or anything, but Barbara would say stuff like "How was your day?" or "What did you do at school?" Then she would wait for the answer and ask follow-up questions, and by then everyone would be talking. At first I tried to get away with one-word responses, but Barbara would just keep looking at me until more words came out.

Occasionally, Dallas would get us weed from his older brother. Until then, I had only ever done whippits behind the Dumpster with Lynn. We would pool our money and go down to the corner store with whatever cash we had managed to squirrel away or steal and buy a couple cans of aerosol whipped cream. We sucked back that nitrous oxide like it was our lifeline out of the neighbourhood. It got less appealing after I saw our neighbour Mimi, a two-litre of glue in front of her nose, staggering through the streets in sock feet with her pants undone. Dallas said his brother was a stoner. We would light up in a pop bottle fashioned into a bong. I got turned on when I smoked weed, and Dallas's qualms about my lack of experience seemed to go out the window after that first time.

I slept over more often than not, and I got up early. I couldn't sleep once the sun was up. Barbara would be down in the kitchen and the coffee would be made. The carafe full to the brim. One morning, I remember I came into the kitchen, and she was very quiet, shuffling around in her slippers, her hair still wrapped in a scarf. I said good morning, poured my coffee, and sat down at the table. I sipped and she came and sat across from me.

"Dallas's dad was a drinker," she said. She said it straight to me. Didn't pretend I was a kid, didn't pretend I didn't know about things. She looked right in my eyes and told me that it had killed him. And then she laughed.

"But he was handsome as hell," she said.

After that we would talk every morning while Dallas and his sister slept. I came down and drank my coffee. Sometimes I would listen to what she was saying and sometimes I would just get lost in how Barbara was looking at me. In the intimacy of the eye contact, in how good it felt to be told about things someone thought I might need to hear.

Barbara was waiting tables at her auntie's restaurant in Hogan's Alley when she met Leonard at seventeen. Hogan's Alley was a thriving Black community at the time, and the restaurant was the heart of it. She told me she wished she could rewind and make it so their paths never crossed. But when it happened it sent a shiver straight down her spine, from her heart to her groin. She was scrubbing down a table for two, wiping the salt and pepper shakers, placing the napkins, the cutlery, and upside-down glasses. He walked in looking so gorgeous she wanted to fall all over him right then and there in the middle of supper service. He came in with Clarence King, who'd been after her for months. But there was something about Leonard that she couldn't resist. He had swagger, he had a bit of cash. He was Italian. A button-up shirt, hair slicked right back, strong tanned hands. She said the first red flag was later that night, when Leonard drank her under the table. Never trust a man who can put it away and still seem stone cold sober. Barbara was so tipsy she could barely stand, but Leonard was witty and sharp as ever. She stumbled as he walked her home, and he put his arm around her waist. She felt how sturdy and warm his body was and she liked it. The two of them spent the rest of the summer in cahoots.

Not long after they met, Barbara was having a smoke break in the alley behind the restaurant and Leonard swept out, half in the bag but charming as hell.

"Barbie Byrne," he said. "I'm gonna kiss you on the goddamn lips." And he did.

They tried to take it further, right there against the side of the building, but Barbara's body clamped down, wouldn't let him in. This should have been the second red flag—that her body physiologically rejected him. In retrospect, she said, she wished her heart had done the same thing.

I don't know exactly what the difference in our skin meant between Barbara and me, or I didn't then. But I knew skin colour was everything in the neighbourhood. As a kid, it was hard to make sense of it. When I was really young, everyone played with everyone. The twins down the street taught me and my brother Cantonese. We all played kick the can. But then at school all the cliques were divided along racial lines. I played Pogs with the three other white girls in my grade at recess and lunch, while the Chinese girls did the same on the other side of the concrete basement. Hopscotch, Tamagotchi, square ball.

The same games but always separate. In high school it got violent. A tough guy showed my brother his machete and threatened to kill him for beating him at badminton, as if the real reason wasn't skin. My brother switched to a white school in a white part of town, right next to the reserve. He and a group of his friends bottled a kid because of his skin outside the 7-Eleven late on a Friday night. They all got caught the way they were bragging. That's how my brother landed in juvie. Not like it was avoidable. That path was laid for him when he was born.

I felt scared walking through my neighbourhood because even though I was white, I was still a skinny kid alone on the strip. An older couple, tourists maybe, gave me a tenner after school one day as I stood outside the smoke shop. The man had a camera looped around his wrist and a tragic expression on his face. I didn't ask for the money. When I got home and looked in the mirror I tried to see what they saw, and I did. Corduroys torn at the knees, bags under my eyes, greasy hair. I leaned in and pulled my lower eyelid down. The white was all red. At the bus stop one morning, I watched a guy on the bench, his hair matted and brown, stick a straw from a juice box all the way up his nose, and then pull it out again, covered in blood and snot. An older girl from school walked past me on my way to Dallas's house late at night and muttered, "Gweilo," even though she was paler than me. Her locker was vandalized with racist slurs the week before, so fair play. An old white dude offered me a twenty for a blow job when I was off my head on whippits. I pretended not to see or hear any of it, but I walked real fast.

I didn't stop doing whippits right after seeing Mimi in the street. Shame wasn't enough to keep me from the sweet bliss of frying my brain cells. Then, one Sunday after Barbara saw me at my worst, she told me to come to church with them. Afterwards, she asked if I wanted to bring my things over and stay with them in a more permanent way.

"Like you're adopting me?" I asked.

"Just don't go telling anyone that," she said.

After their first summer together, Leonard went up north to work in a logging camp and he and Barbara lost touch. Barbara had lovers during those years Leonard was gone. She learned to relax, let people in. But she said part of her was always waiting for him to reappear. And he did. She had moved on from the restaurant, though all the bigwigs still came to eat there. In the time that it was open, her aunt served the best of the best. Ella Fitzgerald and Louis Armstrong, Diana Ross and Sammy Davis Jr., and that's not even half of them.

The summer Leonard came back, Barbara was going to college to become a teacher. She had saved up for two years to pay her tuition. But when she saw Leonard, it was like no time had passed. They were in love, they were on the town, they danced at the club like their feet were on fire. When they slept together, Barbara said it was like nothing she had ever felt before. Like she wanted to fuse herself into him and never come out.

"If we could have melded our bodies together permanently, we would have," she said. "At least in the beginning."

I couldn't help thinking how it wasn't like that with me and Dallas. How I loved him, but we were separate. Maybe that was partly why she was telling me, so I could know what was possible, or maybe what to avoid.

Barbara was three semesters away from being a teacher when she got pregnant, and then they got married. Neither of them had a job, and she had to drop out of school, but they had each other and for a while it was enough. At first Leonard was good. A good dad, a good husband. He worked hard as a valet at the Hotel Vancouver. He didn't drink until after the baby was asleep. But the babies kept coming, and the neighbourhood kept falling apart. By then the rental houses had been torn down, the new highway overpass had been built, and the Black community had scattered. The city called the houses they demolished "blight." It's not a mystery what they were really saying. By baby number three, Leonard would have his first beer at the bar on the way home from work, he'd go straight for the fridge when he walked through the front door, and by the time Barbara was done putting the kids to bed, he was flattened. He got laid off.

Barbara and Leonard ended up in the new projects. Some of the other families kept coming back for church on Sundays, but it was a shift that never set itself right. When Barbara looked around, she thought the neighbourhood was a bunch of sad sacks and drug addicts, single mothers and deadbeat dads roaming the streets too drunk to care whether their kids went to college or ended up like them. I couldn't tell if she was right or wrong. Either way, I wanted out. I wanted to get as far away as I could from the fate Barbara heard knocking at the door.

Eventually, Leonard got work back at the logging camp and would be gone for weeks at a time. Barbara was surprised to find that she was happier without him around, or more calm, more steady. Even though she was lonely, and raising the three kids alone was hard, at least she knew where he was, at least he wasn't staggering up the stairs at all hours, waking the house.

The day he died, she knew what had happened the moment she heard the phone ring. There had been an accident on the work site. Leonard had been drunk. His chainsaw had slipped.

Just before I moved in with Barbara, that same weekend she told me I could stay with them, I went too hard on the whippits. Lynn wasn't around, so I went out alone. I was weightless and falling smoothly to the ground. My body was made of the most sumptuous silk, stuffed with satin, wrapped in fine cashmere and smothered in angora. There was no pain, no hunger, no stiffness, no scratchy throat or bleary eyes. Just pure, lubricated relaxation. It felt like distilled childhood. Like what childhood should be. Like that space between sleep and awake that is slowed right down. Then I was being dragged along a cushioned carpet of velvet, every muscle completely loose. My blood was made of honey. My bones were pliant sponge. I woke to Dallas and Barbara squatting over me, yelling and shaking my shoulders. The world pressed down on my skull like shards of ice, like daggers in my eyes.

"Just five more minutes," I said.

Later, Barbara told me Dallas had found me on the ground, dragged me to the doorstep, and called out to her. My lips had turned purple and I was crumpled up like a rag doll. Barbara said I had stopped breathing. She thought I was dead. She said she prayed that I would wake up, and then I did. I'll never forget how good it felt, before it felt like shit.

Blunt Object

I am running to a destination located on the other side of a large wood. The baby is with me and I am wearing her on my chest. I have nothing else except an axe in a holster on my belt and a water bottle. The trees are dense and tall. Cedars with shaggy trunks. The path is narrow, an obstacle course of roots and rock. It is a two-day run and at the halfway point there is a cabin where we will stay the night before the second leg of the journey. We arrive and I am in good spirits, feeling strong and ready for a nice meal, a shower, and a night's sleep before continuing on in the morning. The cabin is socked in by trees and does not have curtains or blinds on its large windows. It is equipped with only the bare necessities and has an open floor plan. There is a pullout couch in the living room with a picture window, a view of the woods, and a back door to one side. At the other end of the open room is a kitchen, the door to the bathroom, and, down a short hallway, the front door.

I nurse the baby and lay her down on a blanket. I shower, eat, and start to get ready for bed and the second leg of my journey, moving the baby around the cabin as I go. All the lights are on and I feel exposed, even though I know there is no one, not a person or a house, for miles. When the sky darkens, the lights inside reflect off the glass and I am aware of the shadows of trees outside, of how visible I would be if there were eyes looking in. As I make my bed, I see a movement in those shadows. A figure approaching. I move to the back door and find there is no deadbolt, just a lock on the doorknob, which I turn. I test the knob to make sure it's locked. A pathetic defence. I step back from the big window and toward the kitchen. The baby is on the pullout couch and I position myself between her and the door. I watch as the figure approaches. A tall, indistinct shape, broad with shaggy, shoulder-length hair. I remember the axe, but it is too late. I have left it at the front door, leaning against the wall. The knob rattles, stops, then rattles again. The figure shoulder checks the door with a thud, then winds up and shoves again. On the third push, the door gives and she enters the room. She is holding a Swiss Army knife in her hand and gapes at me blankly. Her face is wide and ashen, her shoulders curve forward, and she is hulkingly large. I move backward to the kitchen island and she moves toward me. I don't take my eyes off her, don't dare glance at the baby in case she notices, but search with my hands for something, anything. My fingers wrap around a metal spatula. I run my thumb over the edge and feel that it is blunt, but not so blunt it can't cut. She is close now, just a metre away. Then she is standing in front of me. She tilts her head quizzically and holds the knife up as if examining it. I do not wait. I grasp the spatula by the base of the square and grab the back of her neck. I run the blunt object across her throat once, a second time, and then a third, the cut opening wider with each slice, like a mouth opening to a scream. She frowns at me as though I have offended her. Then she looks at her knife and swallows it whole.

Go Time

I woke abruptly at 4:03 a.m. from a dream in which all my teeth had been replaced by tinned pineapple chunks. When I tried to chew, the pineapple chunks squished out pineapple juice and mushed together like raw flesh. My address growing up was 403 Calver Avenue. Now, I am not usually superstitious, and I am not usually an insomniac, but that was definitely an uncanny coincidence. Last night was Friday night, and also the night of my retirement party. Thirty years of service to Stats Can. They gave me an embossed pen and a cake from Sobeys with a big *30* written on it. When I was thirty, I found out I have a brother. A forty-year-old man who left a message on my answering machine, and then showed up at my door with flowers. It had taken him years to find me. A half brother from my dad, who left the mother, a teenager at the time, high and dry. She had to give up the baby because she was so young, her parents were Irish Catholic, and my dad was nowhere to be found. That baby went on to spend his childhood at the Mount Cashel Orphanage and the adult part of his life dealing with all that. He never explicitly told me he had been abused, but I am making an educated guess. They say that dreams about teeth can mean you have a subconscious fear of failure. I take this dream to mean I ate too much of that Sobeys cake, which was sweet as anything, but subconscious means I am not aware of it, so I could be wrong.

I only met Jacinta once, my first summer on the job. I started as a field interviewer—hammering on doors, asking questions, filling out forms—but I didn't stay in that position for long. Maybe five years. Then I was promoted to supervisor and didn't go door to door much after that. A decade or so later I got promoted to program coordinator, and the past eight years I've been a senior policy analyst. But that one visit that first summer, to Jacinta—that's why I stayed for thirty years. No one at the office knows it, but that was the defining moment of my career.

People ask me, "What will you do with your time now?" as though work is the be-all and end-all, as though finding things to do is some kind of mystery. And I wonder at how dull their lives must be, not to know the answer to that question. Mostly, I will garden and cook. I love dainty flowers, like pansies. They're edible, too. And nasturtiums. Borage. I love tulips, daffodils, crocuses, and hyacinths in spring. The garlic comes up first, and then you know it's go time. Next the lilacs and the rhododendron. In the heat of the summer, it's peonies and roses. And just when you think it's all over, the fall favourites light the yard red. The Prairifire crabapple, the Virginia creeper, and the burning bush. My great pleasure is the garden. And wine. And in the winter, cooking with the preserves I make. Tinned tomatoes, cauliflower pickles, bushberry jam, crabapple jelly. Jim helps me. And he hunts rabbit and moose, which I butcher and store in the deep-freeze, or give away to the neighbours. All this takes time, and now I have it. Retirement also means I will never see Jacinta again, though I figured I never would after she left.

The house where Jacinta lived had fallen into disrepair. Well, strictly speaking, she didn't live in the house. There was moss and tall grass growing in the eavestroughs, and the paint was peeling off the wood siding, which was rotting under the bay window. It was a duplex and the missus living in the upper apartment must have been pushing ninety. She was missing all her top teeth. When Ingrid was a baby, I was shocked when her teeth came in—I didn't think it would be so painful. She would wail and I couldn't figure out what was going on until I would inevitably stick a finger in her mouth as it dawned on me. I would feel around until my finger hit a hard stone of a tooth cutting through. Ingrid is an adult now. Full set of straight teeth, orthodontics paid for by the Blue Cross courtesy of my federal government job. There were perks to Stats Can. Let's just say my pension is very nice.

When I asked the old woman living in the house how many people were in the residence, she told me it was just her. As she was about to close the door, like it was an afterthought, something that just popped into her head, or perhaps like she couldn't quite keep herself from sharing the secret, she told me there was a girl living around back in the shed. Then she pushed the door closed.

As I get older and dentures become a surefire part of my future, I often wonder why we haven't evolved to have a third round of teeth come in at middle age, or even at the end of life. Why our bodies haven't caught up with how long we live now and made it a bit easier on us. When I turned from the old woman's door, I almost left. I almost just went to my car. Part of me did not want to know. But I couldn't resist. I unlatched the side gate, binder clenched under one arm, braced my knees down the mucky hill, and then picked my way through the knotweed and hemlock to the shed hidden at the very bottom of the yard. It was in worse shape than the house. The windows were boarded up. A thick branch from the maple overhead had fallen and caused a whole corner of the shed to cave in. The roof was collapsing under the branch and had sunk all along one side, heavy with moss and rot. There was no one in the shed that day, but I kept going back. I didn't know whether to believe the old woman. She was too spry to have dementia, though, I knew that. Her eyes had too much light.

My brother has met the kids and Jim, of course. Those first years he was around a lot. Less now, but I still see him at holidays, and we call once in a while. My brother told me that the moment he turned sixteen, he signed himself out of the orphanage and took off. He said he was like a wild animal uncaged. He did it all. Sex and drugs, mostly. He lived like a nomad for years before he got the urge to come home, in hostels and on friends' couches, in shelters and tents, and on trains. He took the Amtrak across America, sitting in the viewing car day and night, watching the lakes turn to plains turn to mountains turn to forest. Watching the sky drift by. He said he never imagined the world was so beautiful and he could be so free. A few years ago—oh, maybe even a decade now—I was driving us home from I don't know where. It was late and cold. We were on a residential street in the East End when I saw police lights flashing up ahead. I slowed, as you do, and we watched as four officers took this guy down. He was yelling bloody murder and they were real rough. The guy was shouting and thrashing when one of the officers pulled a spit bag over his head. I had never seen that before, and it made me sick to see a person like that, in handcuffs, four big guys with guns on him, a sack over his head like those prisoners tortured in Guantánamo or Abu Ghraib. My brother told me to keep driving. That was all he said. All the blood was gone from his face and he just stared straight out the windshield.

I went back to the shed every day for two weeks. I went on weekends, evenings, my time off. I was obsessed. I like to think I was a good field interviewer. That I went above and beyond. It didn't even seem like anyone had been in there, until I looked closer. I examined every inch of the place and there were sinister hints. A garbage bag around the back filled with stained rags. The next day it was gone. A patch of grass trodden down where it hadn't been before. A dishcloth hanging from a nail in a tree. The census is a flawed system. We all knew that at Stats Can. But we believed in it, some of us anyway. We knew we could never get everyone, and we knew the ones we missed were always going to be the poorest, the ones who needed most of all to be counted.

The day Jacinta finally came to the door of the shed there was fog and wind. She was feral. Like a wolf, or maybe just like a mother. She was holding a bundle over one shoulder and an axe in her other hand. She looked like she would slit my throat if I took a step toward her.

But then she leaned the axe against the door frame, turned around, and walked back inside. She was barefoot and the floor was dirt. There were spruce boughs laid along the side of the shed with blankets and a pillow overtop. In the corner, an old oil barrel with a hole cut in the side was rigged to a piece of chimney liner sticking out a rotten spot in the ceiling. Jacinta squatted in front of the barrel and stacked kindling in its belly, the baby still clutched to her chest. She struck a match off the metal and the fire caught quick. She filled an old tin kettle from a massive bucket of water before she turned to me.

"Do you want tea?" she asked.

The baby was a month old, Jacinta said. Her name was Sylvia. When I asked where she had given birth, Jacinta did not respond, but her eyes scanned the spruce bough bed, and then down to the baby cradled in her arms. She moved toward the door shortly after that, took my mug from my hands, said how nice it was that I had stopped by. Thinking back now, I might have been pregnant with Ingrid then, without even knowing it, or I was shortly after.

I went back the next day, down the muddy path, through the knotweed and hemlock. I brought diapers and swaddling blankets, a bag of groceries, and a pair of winter boots. When I got to the shed, the door was ajar and everything was gone. The bedding, the spruce boughs, the kettle. The water was drained from the bucket and the oil barrel was cold. I knew I was supposed to call family services. I was supposed to call them the second I left the shed the day before. I was supposed to call them, and I was supposed to go straight back to the office and file a report to my supervisor. Jacinta must have known that, too.

But I didn't, and then, because I had waited, I couldn't. I listened closely at the office when other field workers were chatting over lunch. And for a few months I would sneak into the supervisor's office and leaf through files. When Ingrid started school, I kept my eyes peeled during pickups and drop-offs, or at sports events or community centres or the pool. Sylvia would have been less than a year older than Ingrid. But our paths never crossed. Then it was braces and puberty and birthday parties, and I thought of them less. Though I still listened at work, still watched.

My brother met our dad a few months after he found me. He wanted to hate him, for leaving his mother, for making him an orphan, but my dad was too old to hate at that point. He was in his seventies but seemed older, his voice quiet and cracked, his back bent, his knees giving out. He walked with a cane. My brother is religious. Which always shocks me, given his childhood. He goes to church every Sunday, clasps the hymnal and belts out those songs. The very same songs he sang as a kid, in the very same parish. The very same priests that went at him like carrion fowl.

Maybe I had that dream about the teeth because my favourite dessert is pineapple upside-down cake. Maraschino cherries in the middle of each tinned pineapple round. First you put a load of brown sugar and butter in the pan, and then you lay the pineapple rounds on top, dotting each centre with a burst of cherry red. Then you pour in the batter and bake it. When it comes out, you flip it onto a plate and the brown sugar forms this beautiful glaze over the fruit, making the top of the cake gooey like pudding. I think about Jacinta when I bake, and when I garden. Jacinta, clinging to that axe, fierce as fire.

The Cull

In the weeks leading up to the Vancouver 2010 Winter Olympics there was this fire hydrant that would blast water into the air for twenty minutes every night. It was down by the ocean. When it turned on it would go *burble*, and then *SHHHHH*, as it soared over the seawall from a field by Sunset Beach. I would ride my bike under the flickering archway on my way home from work. Around the same time, a pregnant coyote moved into my spare bedroom. She was small and grey and vicious, and she saved my life.

I was working as a nanny in Coal Harbour for this really rich family. The dad, Paul, was old, sixty-five or something, and he used to be a CEO for Coca-Cola. The mom, Nina, was thirty years younger and from a really loaded Lebanese family that fled to Canada in the eighties during the civil war. They lived in a condo with marble floors that I had to vacuum and mop three times a week. Enamelled lava stone countertops blinked in the sun and windows stretched from floor to ceiling. Everything was white and glossy like photo paper.

Nina and Paul had two kids I looked after. Konstantine and Bella. Only rich people name their kids like that. Konstantine had a cleft palate that barely showed because it didn't go all the way to his lip, but it made him look sharp and churlish. Bella had a perfectly heart-shaped mouth and eyes like sparkling pear cut gemstones.

A few times a week I would stay over at Dylan's house—he was my boyfriend—and in the morning he'd make us porridge for breakfast. He'd always give me a teaspoon to eat with, and I'd always switch it out for a bigger one because I could eat faster. One day he told me that he gave me the small spoon so I would eat less. I was the skinniest I'd ever been when we were dating.

"Slower, but not less," I said.

He said, "I'm just watching out for you."

I could get all the oatmeal down in five minutes with the big spoon. Then I'd race to work on my bike and drive Konstantine to school in the Range Rover, drop Bella off at daycare, and clean the condo from top to bottom. A few months into the job I started taking Adderall. It made me feel like everything I was doing was brilliant and important, even though it sucked. Plus, it killed my appetite.

The day Dylan told me about the spoon, he called me while I was ironing hand towels to say he had scabies. His roommate had picked it up from a German girl he'd brought home who had been staying at a seedy hostel. I had to talk in code on the phone because if Nina and Paul found out I had scabies I would undoubtedly get fired.

"Do I have them?"

"Yeah, probably," he said.

"Oh," I said.

Scabies is extremely contagious. Like, if you have scabies and you touch a doorknob, then the next person to touch the doorknob will definitely get scabies. On my lunch break I went to the pharmacy and bought two bottles of Nix Dermal Cream—that's what you use to kill scabies. In the kids' bathroom at work I took off all my clothes and coated my whole body with the thick white cream from one of the bottles and snuck the contents of the other bottle into the automatic dispenser that held the kids' lotion. The bathrooms were the only rooms in the condo that didn't have surveillance cameras. I stood with my arms out and waited for the cream to sink in before I pulled my clothes back on. Then I used Clorox bleach wipes on every knob, light switch, and surface. When I saw Konstantine playing with his mom's diamond ring I wiped that down, too. After the kids' bath that night I slathered their bodies with Nix. Even between their toes and their butt cheeks. It was the only thing to do, so that the kids wouldn't get scabies, and so that I wouldn't lose my job. They giggled and I prayed they wouldn't tell their parents. Konstantine had eczema anyway, so lotion was a way of life.

When I got off work, I called Dylan to say I couldn't see him until he used Nix, cleaned his house, steam-cleaned the carpets, and put all his clothes in an industrial dryer for at least thirty minutes.

"That's what you have to do," I said. "I don't want to get fired."

He said, "Huh."

I said, "See you in a few weeks."

I rode my bike home under the archway of water that hissed, *SHHHHH*, and twinkled with the city lights. In my room, I piled all my clothes and bedding into garbage bags and went to the laundromat. I spent five hours putting every piece of fabric that could have possibly touched my body in the past month on the hottest setting in the dryer in cycles of thirty minutes.

When I got up the next morning, I noticed that I'd left the window open in the living room, letting in an icy February breeze. I lived in a laneway house, like a granny flat, behind a big house. It used to be a garage, but my landlords had converted it to a stand-alone unit. One bedroom, a kitchen, and a bathroom. I closed the living room window and locked it before going back to my room to get dressed for work. From my closet, there was a strange sound, like *click clack click clack*, and a soft whimper. The sliding closet door was open halfway, and when I moved the mirror along the rails, there was a wiry coyote cowering in the corner with her hackles up. I must have jumped or cursed, and as she moved, I saw that her belly was full and taut, pulling her spine into a bow. She whimpered and shrunk from me, moved her feet up and down as though she were trying to back up, but the wall was behind her. There was a spot on a pile of clean clothes that was flattened down like she had been lying there. I stumbled away from the closet and opened my window wide in case she wanted to leave. She drew her lips up above her teeth and let out a growl. I backed out of the room, closing the door. I remember thinking how small she was. Small and vicious and mangy. I texted Dylan something like, *Hypothetically, what would you do if there was a coyote in your house?* And I texted my boss, *I'm running late, family emergency,* because who would ever believe that there was a pregnant coyote in my bedroom? I looked up the number for the SPCA and googled "coyote in my house Vancouver."

There are lots of coyotes in the city. I used to see them when I was a kid, along the train tracks near my family's house. They kill cats and eat people's garbage. I dialled the number for the SPCA, and while the phone was ringing, I found an article in the *Sun* online that said development for the Olympics was pushing coyotes out of downtown. All the construction and the tourists and the action. I remembered hearing from a friend who worked at Parks Canada that the city had been culling coyotes in secret for at least a decade. Putting poison in their dens. I was on hold with the SPCA, but I hung up and went to the fridge to scrounge together a heaping plate of leftover spaghetti and some rice. I tiptoed back to my room and listened at the door. Silence. I turned the knob quietly and eased inside. I couldn't see the coyote but hoped she was still there. In the closet maybe, or under the bed. I put the plate on the floor and closed the door with a click. My phone buzzed and it was a text from Nina.

I'm sure we won't let this happen again. I'll drop the kids off.

I rushed to work.

When I got down to cleaning that day, all I wanted to do was lie on one of the featherbeds and dream about the coyote. Those beds were clouds. I would stretch the crisp white sheets with like a 10,000 thread count over luxury mattress toppers, and then smooth the duvets wrapped in embroidered white covers overtop. I washed the bedding on Fridays and the parents' sheets always had yellow cum stains that I had to scrub out with Spray 'n Wash before an extra-long cycle in the machine. All the money in the world can't stop cum stains. I couldn't lie down until it was Bella's naptime, and then again when I was putting them both to bed at night, because of the video cameras. Instead, I swallowed an Adderall, chugged a coffee from the inset, wall-mounted espresso machine, put my headphones on, and cleaned, imagining the coyote in my bedroom.

The security preparations in the city for the Olympics had been intense and surveillance helicopters were out in droves. Their chopping was almost constant, and I remember that day specifically. As I was polishing the fingerprints off the glossy cabinets in the kitchen, the automatic timer on the blinds switched on as the sun lifted above the building and they started to rise on the huge picture window behind the dining room table. The window looked out onto the adjacent condos and office buildings and over the ocean to the left. I could hear the beat of the music playing on my phone, but behind it I could hear another faster beat. As the blinds rose, there, low between the buildings, poised so effortlessly, was a helicopter. Just hovering. Its big dragonfly face uncannily close, turned square toward me. I couldn't see the pilot in the glare, just the shiny windows like eyes as it stared into the kitchen. Then, ever so slowly, it lifted itself up above the buildings and flew away.

That night, I stopped by the grocery store and bought a ten-kilo round roast, a package of chicken hearts, and a huge bag of dog kibble. When I got home, the plate of spaghetti was licked clean and I found the coyote in my closet, curled up on the towels, which she had clawed into a nest. She looked up at me without moving her head from her paws, and her black eyes darted to the window. I pulled the blankets and pillows off my bed and slept on the couch.

That week passed in a haze of steam cleaning, Nix treatments, and fried meat. I raced home every day wondering if there would be a litter of puppies waiting. I would creep into my room and the coyote would growl. I would set down a plate of meat, and when I came back in the morning it would be gone. The window stayed open and there was a stinking pile of piss and shit under it. I texted Dylan to say he shouldn't come over because of the scabies. It takes two to three weeks to be sure you're not reinfected. I didn't respond to any of his messages after that.

On the day of the Olympics opening ceremonies, I took Konstantine and Bella to the public library and insisted that they take out a stack of books about coyotes from the kids' section. On the way back to the condo they played "What Time Is It, Mrs Wolf?" and in my head I said, "coyote" instead. On the way home, I rode my bike to the Olympic cauldron on the waterfront and watched the big screen projection of the stadium ceremonies amid a wilderness of overdressed tourists, Roots athletic wear, and kids in protective earmuffs. White plumes of warm breath rose from the throng. I wheeled my bike past a group of protestors, then through the crowd of fans as, onscreen, the former mayor zoomed across the stadium stage in his wheelchair, toting the Olympic flag while the words "Faster Higher Stronger" flowed across a banner behind him. Mascots danced in the background. Cameras flashed in the crowd on the screen like a sparkler, or the shiny flakes of crystal in a piece of granite when the sun catches it at just the right angle. Wayne Gretzky jogged out of the stadium and everyone cheered. When he arrived at the waterfront in the flesh I watched him on the big screen, and then craned to see him in the spotlight, as he held his torch to the base of the cauldron. The flame caught and scrambled to the top.

I checked my phone and saw five missed calls and a text from Nina.

Call me. Urgent.

I struggled out of the crowd and rode home. When I got there, I dialled Nina's number while I opened the door to my room. The coyote was lying in the middle of the floor. She was panting, her stomach heaving, and she looked at me furtively.

"Hello?" Nina said.

"Is everything okay?"

"Hi, yeah, thanks for calling so late," she said. "I hate to say this, but I can't find my Rolex."

"You have a Rolex?" I asked. The coyote whimpered.

"Yeah, I've searched everywhere and I can't find it. Did you see it when you were cleaning today?"

"I've never noticed your watch." I could feel my throat tightening. The coyote squirmed and stood up. She twisted around to her tail, and when I walked toward her, she lay back down and whimpered again.

"The kids haven't seen it and you were the only person here today," she said. "I mean, I'm not accusing you or anything."

I sat down next to the coyote. Her fur was flecked with orange and a million tones of black and grey and white.

"Hello?" Nina said. "Are you listening?"

"Yeah, sorry. I have no idea where it is," I said. "I mean, I wouldn't have moved it even if I did see it."

"Well, we're having a look through the footage from today to see if we can figure it out. I just wanted to talk to you first in case you remembered something."

"I hope you find it," I said.

I rested my hand on the coyote's side and she looked at me out of the corners of her eyes with her ears flattened against her head. She growled soft and low, then looked away. Her fur was coarse and thick between my fingers, and I could feel her ribs. She shifted uncomfortably, lifted her chest off the ground to let out a shrill yelp, then nipped at my hand as she lifted her leg to try and see what was going on. A black bubble was coming out of her. I gasped, she yelped, and I held her hindquarters as she wailed. I grabbed the sac, shimmering like polished obsidian, pulled, and this writhing, encapsulated thing came out. It was slick with black blood. The coyote whipped around and snapped at it. The pouch broke open, and blood was everywhere. She scarfed it all down, peeling the sac off a slimy puppy. My phone buzzed as she bit the umbilical cord and licked the pup clean. I ignored it and watched the tiny pup as it squirmed blindly. The coyote nudged it toward her tummy and it started sucking, like it knew what its job was. Like it knew what was good. I closed the window, turned the heat on, and we waited. I laid out blankets and towels around them. It took three hours for all of the four puppies to come out, and I brought warm water and rags to clean them as they nursed.

On my phone there were three new texts from Nina.

Just so you know the Rolex is worth twenty grand.

If you remember anything just give me a call.

Then:

Watching footage now, still no luck.

I called her back and it went to voice mail. I tried to remember if there could possibly be anything on the video footage about the scabies fiasco. The coyote was lying on her side on the bloodied blankets, her four pups suckling and squirming as she recovered. I fell asleep on my bed. At one o'clock, my phone rang and it was Nina.

"Guess what?" she said.

I kept my eyes closed.

"We watched the footage," she said.

I snapped awake.

"This morning Bella was lying on my bed and she picked the watch up off the bedside table." Nina was laughing now. "Guess what she did with it?"

"What?"

"She hung it on the switch under the lampshade. You know, the switch to turn the lamp on. So funny." I didn't laugh and it was silent. "She hung it there and forgot, and when we looked, it was still there. God, we were cracking up watching her on the tapes."

Nina paused, then: "Why are you awake anyways?"

"I have to go," I said, then clicked the red circle and collapsed into sleep.

I didn't go back to work after that, even though I wanted to tell Konstantine and Bella about the coyote and watch their faces contort in awe. Later that week, I texted Dylan to say it was over. He said he wanted to see me, and I said I needed some distance. I only saw him once after that, months after the Olympics were over, when the lineups of sports fans in red mittens had gone back to Russia or Korea or Scandinavia and the streets were empty again.

I was riding the SkyTrain home, and even though it was cold out, I was sweating because it's always so hot on the train. I was wearing headphones, and when I stepped onto the escalator going up, there was Dylan's face at the top coming toward me, next to a girl I couldn't look at. Our eyes met and he nodded and said, "Hi," as though we were just acquaintances, just passersby on our usual weekend transit route. He passed so close that our knuckles almost touched. I could have leaned over and smelled the way he didn't wash his hair. I wanted it all to slow down long enough that I could reach out, long enough that I could curl my fingers over the cold edge of his ear. My heart was pounding in my throat as he slipped by.

The coyote was long gone by then. She had stayed until the pups were big enough to play and bite. The fire hydrant stopped spraying across the seawall, and I woke one morning to find my house empty, the living room window open wide, and the curtains billowing in the wind.

The Weight of It

I approach the memorial in chunky black platforms. Sandals with a thick heel and wide elastic straps. A silver buckle on the arch. I am wearing lipstick to honour the dead. The memorial is just down the street from my house. Or maybe it's your house. Maybe it's everywhere. The atoms of all the bodies dispersed into everything. A diaspora. Armed guards stand as sentinels. It is unclear if they are there to protect or intimidate, with their rifles and tight haircuts, though I have my suspicions. It is important to remain inconspicuous. If at all possible, it is a good idea to hide behind a shield of sun-damaged and freckled skin. Your own, or a friend's. My grandmother told me to hide my tattoos, and I have worn long sleeves to appease her. In the shadow of these guns, I am grateful for her advice. As I walk by the memorial, guards stare and ghosts wail. My body is leaden. I can feel sorrow pressing in. My limbs are drawn to the ground by the magnetic weight of this place. My hands drag on the concrete. My knees bend and bear me down, the weight of my hips unsupportable as they grind to a halt in their sockets. My cheerful shoes become an iron fist. The air is sucked out of my lungs and their walls collapse. My cheek presses into the pavement and I feel the sharp bumps of it tearing at my skin. My throat slumps, tongue lolls. My eyelids, then red lips, pull off and melt into the sidewalk like toffee. I do not go in but walk on and home.

Be Happy Darling and Love Me

The first time Lou and Daria slept together they were having a dance party in the basement. MDMA was floating around in mini parachutes of toilet paper and everyone was high, washing it down with beer from a keg that was so hard to pump you broke a sweat. Lou was making out with someone in drag, then the next minute he had his hands up Daria's shirt and a boner like a can of Coke on an airplane. Daria was short and rectangular. She had curly ginger hair and lopsided breasts like plums that stared out cockeyed through her tank top. Her armpits smelled strongly of onions. When she was on top of Lou, her boobs swished from side to side. Lou stared at Daria's tits and wondered if he could fit one in his mouth completely. After that night, they partied and wrote term papers and accidentally screwed the semester away. Somewhere in the middle of it, Lou's grandfather died.

Bernie was eighty-five. He had been moved out of the home he'd shared with his wife, Laila, and into Meadowbrook Seniors Residence some years before. Bernie's death was drawn out and painful, starting with the slow burn of Alzheimer's. But the last part went quick: aspirated vomit, pneumonia, septicemia, and a week later he was dead. Laila was younger than Bernie by thirteen years. Even in her old age, she hadn't lost her bright kitten eyes, high cheekbones, and sharp jaw. Her parents had come to Canada from Ukraine. Bernie's family came from Belarus, before the Soviet invasion of Poland.

The night everyone realized Bernie needed to move into an old folks' home was terrible. Lou was fifteen. His grandmother phoned and his mom answered. Lou could picture Laila in her nightie, maybe with curlers in her thin hair. She would have had her makeup off, dentures out, cheeks sagging and soft where her teeth had been, making her cheekbones look even sharper, hands trembling. Lou's grandfather had decided he was a young man. When Laila came out of the bathroom, ready for bed, teeth soaking on the counter in a glass of Polident, Clinique cream liberally applied, Bernie cried out in terror, slammed the bedroom door in her face, and locked it. On the phone, Lou's mom could hear him in the background.

"I know what you want, you old hag!" he yelled. "Take your rotting pussy somewhere else."

The diatribe continued, fouler and fouler. Laila was weeping, pleading. Bernie kept spitting insults.

Much later that night, when Bernie finally unlocked the bedroom door and ventured out, the lights were all off. He wandered through the house calling out in a whisper, "Laila, Laila." He couldn't remember why he had been so scared. He could just make out her silhouette in the hallway. She was hesitant. She asked if he was okay, and he said of course he was. She asked if she could come in the bedroom, and he said he wanted to go to bed.

Daria's mom's family hadn't been able to leave Europe before the war. They were all killed, except her grandmother, who survived the Vaivara concentration camp in Estonia. She was sixteen when the war ended. She managed to get out to California, where she lived with a cousin. She met a rich guy who had fled his Orthodox upbringing and made it big in the early days of the tech industry. They had kids young. No one in Daria's family went to synagogue. Daria described them like Seth Cohen's family on *The O.C.* They celebrated Chrismukkah and sent their kids to a secular private school in Malibu. Her parents had wanted Daria to go to university, but she didn't get in anywhere in the States, so she applied in Canada.

Lou's dad was Korean and an atheist. He'd tried his best to appease Lou's mother's family by converting when it was clear they would be marrying. They accepted him once he was Jewish, but only because they would have to admit the extent of their prejudice if they didn't. When Lou's grandfather went to war in the forties, he had an office job. They were called the Royal Canadian Army Service Corps. Bernie was stationed in Ontario, and then in Belgium, and then in the Netherlands. His letters to Laila during that time always ended something like this:

Oh darling. I want so much to be with you—holding and loving you. I dream of it constantly. Babes, darling, I love you and need you so much. But soon the hurt of missing you will be gone. Good night, my sweet—love me, baby—All my love, Toodles

Never anything salacious, never any mention of the horrors of war, of the fear he must have felt as people just like him were being massacred. Once he wrote to her about buying her lingerie in Paris—that was as risqué as he got. And that Toodles. Other words Lou's grandfather was prone to using before his Alzheimer's set in were "thingamabob" and "doohickey." His love for Laila was legit. He did whatever she said. "Don't eat the sugar cookies, they're bad for your diabetes." "Okay, hon." "Bring the dog out before she shreds the couch." "Okay, babes." Frankly, it was incongruous to imagine him yelling about her rotting pussy, but it really happened. Lou's mom heard it, word for word.

It was also confounding that Lou and Daria kept at it. He didn't like her personality, and she was annoyed by his very presence in a room. They were simultaneously attracted to and repulsed by each other. Her body odour was pungent and sour, but the pheromones were primed for Lou's brain. And they did a lot of drugs together, only ever socially, but social time was most of the time, so it became a habit.

Lou and Daria lived with a third roommate, Kurt, in a house just off Commercial, not far from the row house where Lou had grown up. Kurt was a WASP, of the watered-down atheist type from a secular Christian family. He was born in the city, had grown up in a fancy house in West Point Grey. Kurt wore vintage suit pants with suspenders and smoked cigarettes with his legs crossed at the knobbly knees, flicking the ashes lazily into the carpet. He was an intellectual—or he looked like one—tall and thin and pointy all over. When the three of them smoked a joint together that first night after they moved in, Lou thought even Kurt's dick must be pointy.

Lou had only ever taken small quantities of ketamine, but Kurt sold him a bag of it for cheap. He said he liked to do a bit and read Kant or Proust, which sounded like total bullshit. Lou stored it with his socks. He and Daria dabbled, a bump here and there after a long day. They agreed that it didn't actually feel very good. But then Lou started seeing Bernie when he was high and he couldn't stop.

Hallucinations are common on ketamine, or special K, or K. The forums say hallucinations are definitely a thing. Though Lou could not help thinking that it really was Bernie's ghost, and the K was just the medium for the apparition. Bernie would just stand there. Sometimes in Lou's room. Sometimes in the kitchen. He would stare at Lou and gesticulate slowly, lips moving. But it was impossible to hear what he was trying to say. Like he was on mute, moving in slow motion. Lou would get really close up to his mouth, and still, nothing. He could smell Bernie's breath and feel the heat off him. A line of white crusty spit rimmed the inside part of his lips. His teeth were yellowed. But no matter what Lou did, he couldn't hear him. When Bernie would appear like this, he wasn't super old. Not like he was just before he died. More like how Lou remembered him before he got Alzheimer's. Maybe seventy, still lucid and not yet hunched over. Pretty fit, even. And it really seemed like he was trying to say something important. Sometimes Lou thought he could read Bernie's lips, but all he could make out was "doohickey" and "thingamabob," but really slow. And then Lou would start laughing and Bernie would leave.

In the haze of that winter Lou totalled his car. He and Daria were messed up on K and Lou was driving. He didn't think he had taken a big dose and suddenly Daria was undoing his pants and going down on him in heavy traffic. The air got really heavy, like the molecules were so dense he could barely move. Or like his body was lighter than air, like his muscles didn't stand a chance against the weight of it. There was a hearse up ahead, cars bumper to bumper. A funeral procession must have been going over the Burrard Street Bridge because everyone had their emergency lights going and they were all blinking in sync to the rhythm of Daria's head bouncing in Lou's lap. At first, everything was overwhelmingly warm. Lou could see his hands on the steering wheel, but he couldn't feel them like usual. They were tingling like their souls had floated up out of them and left these shells behind, still in charge of a car. He looked ahead as the road started to spread over the entire windshield. Then the road was like a soft polyester blanket at a motel. It wrapped him up and everything was muffled. The world ground to a halt. The concrete grey of the road was everywhere, and everything lost its edges and blended into him. He was nothing and the whole universe was nothing. As Lou watched Daria's head bobbing up and down, slowly, like it was full of helium, like their bodies were full of helium, his hands melted off the steering wheel, the right one onto Daria's back, the left one into the abyss beside him. They were two big pink mitts full of helium, floating down. And then he drove into the guardrail on the bridge and he was so high he didn't do anything about it. There was cum everywhere, filling up the car, melting into him, and he had no idea what was going on.

Lou didn't visit his grandpa even once when he was sick, just before he died. It wasn't a conscious decision. But he went to his grandfather's room at Meadowbrook the day after he was gone and took the box of letters Bernie and Laila had written to each other while Bernie was in the war. The room was still stuffy with the smell of Bernie's body. Lou opened the bottle of aftershave sitting on the dresser and breathed it in. He opened the window to let in some air and let out whatever vestiges of Bernie were still lingering.

After the car crash, Lou stopped doing ketamine and Bernie's ghost stopped visiting. But late one night, sober and alone, Lou started reading the war letters. His grandparents were so formal with each other but so in love. Laila would say things like:

> *Darling, I don't have to tell you how much I love you, and even if I did, I probably couldn't because there are no words to describe the amount. Someday soon I hope to be able to show you.*

And Bernie would sign off like:

> *Each day I bless my luck in having you. You're alone, and beyond anything I deserve, but I'm going to make myself deserving of you. Good night, Laila mine, I'm so in love with you. Be happy darling and love me.*

Power Pose

I see the local coke dealer in the bar, and I see him walking on my street. In the summertime, I see him riding a bike I sold him on Kijiji down a steep hill with his backpack on. Am I complicit because I sold him the bike? I serve him in the café and he orders oolong tea.

I meet a woman who has moved here from Toronto. She comes into the café hungover and we chat for half an hour as I hold a bussing tray. At first I wipe the tables around her while we talk, and then I just stand there listening, a rag wet with Windex in my hand. She is hungover, but she is also still high and I can smell the booze on her breath. The hangover dims her face to grey. I want to wipe it away so I can see what she really is. She tells me about her life in Toronto. She asks me if I've got a tampon she can have. She tells me that she hasn't been home yet because she's trying to leave her boyfriend. She tells me she is trying to leave him because he has been pimping her out to his friends and taking the money to buy blow. Later that day I see her walking down the street with the coke dealer and a local author who writes grungy novels that everyone says are authentic and unveil the dark side of this town. He hasn't actually lived here for decades. He left for a chic life in the big city. I wonder if he is hanging out with the dealer and the woman from Toronto because he is doing research, or if they are friends, or maybe it is a business transaction, maybe the research is later.

I see the author alone, walking his Shih Tzu. I am standing next to a statue of the author's father, who was also an author, who everyone loved and maybe reviled, and who died slowly of organ failure brought on by drinking. The statue smells like piss from drunken revellers. The author walks up to the statue with his Shih Tzu. He kisses the pads of his fingers and places his hand on his father's knee. He closes his eyes and stands like that. I walk away.

At a party I see the woman from Toronto. She is fresh and renewed. I follow her to the living room and she is beautiful. She sparkles gold and smells like tapioca pudding.

She says, "Hey, I know you from the café," and holds out her hand. "I'm Alice," she says. She is sober and different. She tells me she is a photographer and to follow her on Instagram. The coke dealer comes into the room and she waves at him, says excuse me, and leaves.

At home that night, I scroll through Alice's profile. As it turns out, she is Instagram famous for her seductive self-portraits. She plays the virgin whore in pink satin, clutching a dagger or tied up in leather. She has over a million followers. She's vocal and eloquent in her captions about past experiences with sexual assault and reclaiming her sexuality. I google her and find out she shows her work in galleries.

She has a piece at the AGO. She plays with dominance, submission, and self-portraiture to create what some critics are calling "a brilliant commentary on sexual power in the time of the #MeToo movement," and others are calling "vapid, pornographic exploitation of a powerful moment in feminism." The photos are affecting either way, and sexy as hell. I try to make sense of it all, with the incoherent conversation we had at the café and the things she told me about her boyfriend.

I click back to Instagram. The photos are washed out, with a short depth of field. Everything in the background is blurry, but there is an acute focus in the foreground. The colours are pastel and desaturated. Some of the photos have ornate backdrops like Renaissance paintings: luxurious draped silk, exotic bouquets, a bowl overflowing with fruit, a parrot on a perch. Others are just her body in a stark white room. I click Follow, then scroll. In one photo she is on all fours with her ass to the camera, looking over her shoulder with a rhinestone studded gag in her mouth and her ankles bound. In the next she's standing in a power pose, wearing vintage cat-eye sunglasses and black leather, wielding a switchblade. In the next she's topless except for a powder-pink chest harness, staring straight into the camera with her lips moist and parted, arms pressed against her boobs. A photo of the fold of her hip, lavender satin thong, a mole on the edge of the frame. Alice holding two open pocket knives, blades covering her nipples. She is looking down at the camera, curls tumbling around her face. Every once in a while she posts a really short video of her body moving. Her waist flexing into a stretch or arching backward. I'm turned on and click my phone screen off.

The author with the Shih Tzu is up for a big award. This must be why he's in town—there are readings and a gala. I wonder if I'll see him again. I wonder what his connection is to Alice. Fame and art, or drugs, or something more intimate. I go out in search of him, wandering the streets to locations where I have seen him. I try to understand my obsession. That's what it has become, I think, an obsession. Something about the way he stood by the statue with his eyes closed—I wanted to take him in my arms. But maybe it was purely self-serving—the obsession, that is. Maybe I just wanted him to take me into the inner fold. On my travels, I see the drug dealer. I see Alice and say hi. I continue to look for the author. On Instagram, Alice messages me and tells me she's having an art show at a gallery downtown. She invites me to the opening, says she is giving an artist talk and would love to see a friendly face in the crowd. I say I would love to go and note how lonely she must be to have invited me as though we are great friends when we barely know each other.

At the gallery, Alice is luminous. At the end of her talk there is a question period and in the pause before her first answer, she crosses her arms and frowns. One lone crease carves between arched eyebrows. I can barely focus on what she's saying when her answer comes.

Later, I'm standing by the cheese plate, searching the room. I'm holding my wine as my eyes crest the tops of heads and finally settle on Alice's. I move toward her, saying only quick hellos to people I know. I put my wineglass down on the table just next to her. She's chatting with the curator and another man. I think for a moment the other man is the author and I catch my breath, but when he turns it's the coke dealer. Alice is drinking a glass of red wine, which she moves gracefully as she speaks and gestures with the other hand, smooth and confident. She has done this before: talked to big groups, held the attention of a room. Her every movement is practised.

"It's just such a basic critique of sexuality," she says. "It lacks nuance."

I pick up my wine again, clutching the glass as I bring it to my lips carefully, as though it might get away from me if I don't hold it that tightly. I made the mistake of taking a puff of someone's joint outside. I'm bad at weed and suddenly panic about how stilted my wine drinking must seem. Alice stops talking and looks at me, hovering there on the edge of their conversation.

"Joanie," she says, as she reaches out to hold my face, kissing me tenderly on either cheek. "It is so good to see you."

She introduces me to the curator and the coke dealer. She calls him, simply, Mike.

We talk for an hour. Mostly, I listen. The curator and Mike fall into their own conversation, and Alice and I step closer to each other. I tell her that I'm a writer, that I've written for *Vice* and *McSweeney's*, a few local culture blogs. The job at the café pays the bills. I relax a bit. I think how this all sounds pretty good, like I, too, am credible and confident. I try to focus on eye contact and active listening, though my brain is still struggling to make smart sentences because of the weed. Alice leans in and whispers in my ear that she hates gallery talks—it's all such an act. She says it as a disclosure, a secret between us, her breath warm on my cheek. She brushes my hair to the side, her fingertips grazing my temple, sliding behind my ear, and then along the nape of my neck. This is her first solo show of this size and she says she's nervous. I meet her eyes and try on my most sympathetic expression. She invites me to her place at the end of the month. When the show closes she's having a party, a few friends, she says.

It's hot out and I wear jean shorts and a leopard-print blouse to the party. When I arrive, Alice answers the door holding a dachshund under her arm she introduces as Peter Pan. She is wearing a violet mohair sweater. It's short and I can see the tiniest slice of skin between her shirt and pastel plaid skirt. She's wearing knee socks and her hair is pinned back on both sides. I am struck by how fancy her apartment is. I don't think she's much older than me—eight years, maybe ten at most—but she's in a different world. Somehow, she has lots of money. Maybe that's all her art is about, making money. I give her the bottle of wine I brought. She brings me past an expansive vinyl collection and shining glassware to the kitchen. A gas range and one of those fancy industrial stainless steel hood fans. She pours us both a glass of wine and gives me a tour. I can hear a few people in the living room, but she brings me to the back of the apartment first. It is surprisingly filthy. The floor in her room is scattered with clothes. In the bathroom, the claw-foot tub has a ring of soap scum. The lights are dimmed in the hallway, but it doesn't hide the dust on the baseboards and in the corners. She fills my glass again in the kitchen and we go to the living room. When I walk in, I am curious to see so few people, a handful of familiar faces from the gallery. Among them, the person I had most hoped to meet. I break a sweat. The author is there, sitting on the couch, talking quietly to Mike.

Alice has made a spread of vegan finger food, laid out at the side of the room with a large selection of alcohol. There is hummus drizzled with oil and topped with a sprinkling of paprika, endives with olive tapenade and shiny pomegranate seeds, stuffed mushroom caps, fried cauliflower with cashew cream.

"The secret is the nutritional yeast," Alice says, pointing to the cashew cream.

I recently watched a documentary about the horrors of cashew processing, but I don't mention it. As I spear a crispy cauliflower chunk with a toothpick and dip it in the cream, I imagine the fingers of the women peeling the cashews, burnt black by the acid from the shells.

As I'm chewing, the author approaches. My cheek is full and I nod a salutation. He and Alice want a cigarette, they decide. She wraps an arm around my waist and we step outside. I don't smoke, so I sit on the bench as they flick the lighter and inhale. Alice's arm is around her own stomach now, the other propped up and the cigarette poised between her fingers, her chin jutting forward as the smoke shoots above her, then flattens against the low roof over the front stoop. I watch a large mint-green moth flutter around the light. The night is warm and smells of grass and cherry blossoms. On this porch the world is calm. Alice and the author talk quietly, and then the author sits beside me.

"I've seen you around," he says. He tells me his name, which of course I already know. I shake his hand and hope that I seem cool and aloof rather than stunted and meek. I look for the moth, but it's gone.

Alice drifts above us. "Look at that moth on your thigh," she says.

I turn my gaze down, and sure enough, it's resting there, bright against my skin, wings spread flat. It has white veins running out from its body, thinner than thread. It is the colour of jadeite, of hospital bathrooms and the 1950s, retro hand mixers and rotary phones. The texture of a Mentos, powdery and matte. It flutters and then relaxes again. It feels like eyelashes blinking against my leg.

I look at the author staring at the moth. I wonder if he is staring in awe of this fragile thing. I wonder if he will write about this later. Suddenly, he raises his hand and slaps it down hard on my thigh. When he removes it, there is a smear of pale green dust. I feel my stomach knot as he laughs. Mike pops his head out the front door.

"Let's go to the bedroom for a bit," he says, and turns back inside. The author gets up, wiping his palm on his pants.

"That was messed up," Alice whispers, before taking my hand and pulling me after her.

In the bedroom, the author cuts lines on the glass-topped desk, which is covered in Alice's stuff. A hairbrush full of hair. An open lipstick tube on its side, red smudges on the glass. A pair of dirty underwear in a ball, a crusty smear visible on the black cotton crotch. Mike is lying back on the bed, scrolling on his phone. The author swivels around on the square vintage office chair and gestures to the neat strips of white he has arranged for us all.

After, Mike leaves to make a delivery. The author excuses himself and kisses Alice on the lips. He closes the door behind him. Alice starts pulling clothes out of her closet and instructs me to try them on. My head is buzzing. She hands me a baby pink silk negligee trimmed with lace. A cream waist-length sheer cape. I pull off my clothes and step into hers. She hands me her vintage cat-eye sunglasses and I place them on my face. Her mirror is spattered with makeup and flecks of dried liquid. When I look at myself through the filth, I am shocked to see a hybrid version of us both. Alice gets her camera and takes pictures. She directs me on how to move, and then she tells me to take the clothes off.

She puts the camera on the bed and slips a black chest harness over my head, slides the strap under my boobs. She ties my hands behind my back with a long silk scarf. It is violet with white pinstripes. So innocent. But when she knots it, it's tight and cuts the circulation to my hands. She places a ball gag in my mouth, fastens the collar behind my neck. I'm still wearing the cat-eye sunglasses and I stand there naked. She puts a hand on my shoulder, guides me to my knees. As the carpet digs into my skin, I try not to think about how dirty the room is.

Acknowledgments

Like all books, this one relied on so many people, places, and years. I am very grateful for the community I had as a kid and teenager in the DTES and Strathcona that inspired much of this book. And for St. John's, the gift of living and writing in this shock of a town. I started writing these stories as the long-standing overdose crisis accelerated and finished writing at its current horrifying peak. Thank you to everyone keeping people alive, and curse the forces that have let so many we love die.

Thank you to Stephanie Sinclair for believing in my work and finding this book of stories the perfect home. Thank you to everyone at Arsenal Pulp Press—to Brian Lam for enthusiastically publishing this collection; to my editor, Shirarose Wilensky, for so staunchly supporting this work, for reading it so closely and kindly, and for making it so much better; to my publicists, Cynara Geissler and Jaiden Dembo; and to Jazmin Welch for the design of the book. So much admiration and gratitude for Janice Wu, who creates beautiful art. I am honoured to have such a book cover.

To my parents, Joyce Cosgrove, who taught me to love reading, and Stephen Gray, who showed me how to be a writer. You are at the heart of everything. Thank you for crawling into bed with the baby so I could crawl out. Thank you also to Mary and Leonard Mandville, John Cosgrove and Patrice Potvin for caring for my child, and for me. This book would not exist without the hundreds of hours you have given. To Isaac, Louisa, and Tilley, thank you for your love and for bringing me to the mausoleum of Emanuel Vigeland.

So many thanks to my chosen family, Susie Taylor, the first to read every story in this collection and more, and Colleen Soulliere. You are the best cooks and the best friends. I am so thankful to my friend Eva Crocker for your invaluable feedback and support. Thank you to Kym Greeley for sharing New Chelsea and for your generous friendship. To Nina Gustafson for sustaining me in the hardest times and Elise Thorburn for sticking with me. Thank you to Lisa Moore, who told me to keep writing. You changed my life. And to Sharon Bala for your encouragement and insightful edits.

Writing this book—and also eating—was possible because of financial support from the Canada Council for the Arts and ArtsNL. Thank you to the Banff Centre for Arts and Creativity, where I finished this collection, and to Zoe Whittall for offering to blurb this book before it was done, over Skype at the start of a pandemic. Thank you to earlier editors of some of these stories, including Emma Cleary, Crystal Mackenzie, Sofia Mostaghimi, Pamela Mulloy, and Claire Wilkshire.

I am so thankful for my muses: my dearest and oldest friends Erica Forssman, Danica Doyle, Jessie McNeil, Hannah Spaulding, and Cisca Harrison; Katherine Loewen, the ultimate partner in mischief, who left this world too soon; and my grandmothers, Marie-Paule Veilleux and Freda Gray, whose lives are half mystery, half everything I've ever known.

Thank you to Aubrey Mars, my darling, for teaching me about the fleeting nature of time and the overwhelming expanse of love. Most of all, thank you to David, Mandy, LABF, for everything and forever. I would be exactly nowhere without you.

Photo credit: David Mandville

Carmella Gray-Cosgrove was raised in the Downtown Eastside of Vancouver and lives in St. John's, on Ktaqmkuk, with her partner and their child. Her fiction has appeared in *PRISM international*, *Broken Pencil*, the *New Quarterly*, the *Antigonish Review*, and elsewhere. *Nowadays and Lonelier* was shortlisted for the NLCU Fresh Fish Award for Emerging Writers. She was the 2020 writer-in-residence for *Riddle Fence* magazine. Carmella holds a master's degree in geography from Memorial University and was an F.A. Aldrich Fellow.